'You mustn't cross Black Edward!' urged the old woman, her eyes wide. 'If that compass is his, you must give it back. And you must give it to him!' She seized one of their hands in each of her spindly ones. 'You saw the ghost ship, you say? That means he's back – Black Edward Sharksbane! He'll be coming to the island, to take what's his – and what isn't.

'And when he comes, you have to promise me. Promise me you'll stay away from him! Or he might not ever let you go…'

Mysteries of RaVeNSTORM IsLand

THE SHIP OF GHOSTS

GILLIAN PHILIP

ORCHARD

ORCHARD BOOKS
338 Euston Road, London NW1 3BH
Orchard Books Australia
Level 17/207 Kent Street, Sydney, NSW 2000

First published in the UK in 2015 by Orchard Books

ISBN 978 1 40833 020 3

A CIP catalogue record for this book is available
from the British Library.

1 3 5 7 9 8 6 4 2

Printed and bound in Great Britain by CPI Group (UK) Ltd, Croydon, CR0 4YY

The paper and board used in this book are made from wood from responsible sources.

Orchard Books is an imprint of Hachette Children's Group, and published by
The Watts Publishing Group Limited, an Hachette UK company.

www.hachette.co.uk

*For Jamie, who had early experience as a pirate
and is now an ace (and lawful) sailor*

Ravenstorm Hall was outlined so sharply against a dazzling blue sky, Molly Cornell could count every single gargoyle crouched on its great parapet. Shading her eyes, she smiled up at the grotesque stone figures among the turrets and spires, then glanced at her little brother Jack to make sure he was distracted. Sure enough, he was checking the contents of his beach bucket yet again.

'Shovel, rake, fork,' he muttered. 'Rake, fork, shovel…'

'The gargoyles are all there for now, Arthur,' Molly whispered to her cousin with a wink, nodding up at the hall's roofline. 'Every single one!'

Mornings this beautiful, and unspoilt by mist, were rare on Ravenstorm Island; Molly and her little brother Jack had only been staying here for two weeks with their cousin and aunt and uncle, but she was already familiar with the ever changing weather. Over the last few days, with their constant drizzle, she and Arthur and Jack had had plenty of fun exploring the hall's vast rooms and dark corridors. It had been undeniably exciting to prowl through locked rooms full of barely readable ancient books, climb spiral staircases swagged with cobwebs, and to discover unexpected cabinets full of treasures, tucked away in shadowy passageways. Still, now that the weather had changed, they were all too glad to be up early for a day out of doors. Molly thought she could happily spend all the long days swimming and exploring the beach and the deep woods and the overgrown, enticing grounds of the hall. Until the clouds rolled in again, anyway.

'I like to see all those gargoyles on parade,' said Art. In a whisper Jack couldn't hear, he added,

'Even the ones that sometimes go wandering…'

Molly grinned at her cousin, thinking of the secret they shared about Ravenstorm Hall's craggy butler… But Jack tugged impatiently at her arm.

'Come *on*, Moll!' he demanded. 'I thought we were going to the beach!'

'Indeed we are, Magic Boy.' Taking his hand, Arthur waved cheerfully to his parents on the great front steps of the hall, and Jack followed his example.

'Bye, Uncle Bill! Bye, Aunt Catherine! Bye, baby Harriet!' Pulling his hand out of his cousin's, he strode off determinedly, swinging his bucket, so fast that Molly and Arthur had to jog to catch up. He clearly wasn't settling for any more delays.

'Have a wonderful time at the beach!' shouted Uncle Bill after them.

'And don't get into any trouble!' called Aunt Catherine, jiggling the squalling Harriet in her arms.

'If only you knew, Mum,' murmured Art, and Molly giggled.

Sun dappled the winding, laurel-shaded drive of

Ravenstorm Hall, already blazingly warm though it was only nine o'clock. On a morning like this, thought Molly with a thrill in her spine, it would be easy to forget the creatures she knew haunted the island, from malevolent mermaids to trolls, and the mysterious creature that was said to live in Art's garden pond.

And not forgetting the Shadowprye, thought Molly. In her mind's eye she saw their strange dark realm which she and Art had entered through the cave beneath the roots of the great gnarled oak tree on the cliffs. Molly felt a shiver as the pictured the spindly winged creatures, armed with thorn spears – and magic powerful enough to turn all the children of the island to stone. No, she certainly wouldn't forget them in a hurry, Molly thought.

Arthur gestured with a thumb at the row of gargoyles. 'So Mason's back in his place,' he said, free to speak more loudly as Jack ran ahead. 'Maybe he decided he could have a nap, since the island's nice and peaceful again.'

'For now!' laughed Molly. They'd been quite startled to discover that the Wolfreys' morose family butler was in fact a living gargoyle – but perhaps, after their adventures with the island's angry Sprye, not as shocked as they might have been.

'I can't help hoping it won't be *too* quiet,' said Arthur mischievously. 'That might be a bit boring, after we saved all the island children from being statues forever.'

'Shh! Jack'll hear you!' Molly was sure her little brother didn't remember being turned to stone, but she didn't much want to jog his memory.

She couldn't help agreeing with Art, though. After all, Molly had always wanted magic to be something more than the sleight of hand and tricks with conjuring props her parents used in their show. Every summer the Incredible Cornells toured the country, leaving Molly and Jack with friends or relatives. Her aunt and uncle's new home of Ravenstorm Hall had to be her parents' best choice yet – because here Molly had discovered there *was* real magic in the world.

Even though it'd been pretty scary, she hoped she hadn't seen the last of it. The Shadowsprye magic had stolen the island children away and turned them into stone statues, and Miss Badcrumble's magic had made all the adults forget they'd ever had children. She'd meant well, only wanting to spare them the pain of losing their children, but her magic had meant that when Jack went missing, Aunt Catherine and Uncle Bill refused to believe he had ever existed.

The hall's leaf-shadowed drive had opened out into wide, tree-lined lanes, and after half a mile they glimpsed the roofs and chimneys and the distinctive church spire of Crowsnest, the island's main village. A steep, knee-jolting road brought them at last to Main Street. It seemed busier today, with tourists and locals hurrying in and out of shops, eating ice creams or taking photographs of the prettiest gardens and cottages. As Jack dashed ahead, Arthur waved at Mrs Chambers, who had poked her head out of her craft shop for a breath of fresh air and sunshine.

'Good morning,' she shouted, creasing her eyes

against the sun as she shoved her wispy hair out of them. 'Isn't this beautiful for a change?'

'Morning, Mrs C,' Molly and Art shouted in unison, and Molly added, 'Isn't it nice?'

'Off to the beach? Lucky things!'

Arthur grinned and waved again in farewell as Jack came pelting back to their side.

'There's Kelp Street. Hurry up, Molly!' Once again he raced off.

'Is he excited, do you think?' asked Arthur dryly as they turned down Kelp Street, a winding cobbled lane that led all the way to the beach. Despite the steep slope, there was sand between the cobbles, and straggles of dry black seaweed had been flung far up the road by storms. 'Wow. The sea must come a long way up!'

'Maybe it happened in the bad weather last week,' suggested Molly. 'No wonder Jack's over-excited – I thought we'd never see the sun again all summer!'

'Nah,' said Arthur. 'It hasn't been stormy enough for all this seaweed to be washed up this far – just miserable and wet. I hope it stays like this now.' He tilted his face happily to the sunlight. 'I want to explore a lot more of the island.'

'Oh, me too.' Molly grinned as the road petered out and they jumped down into the sand, then kicked off their shoes. Jack had started digging a hole down by the water's edge, but was almost immediately distracted by a nearby rock pool. Flopping onto his stomach, he gave a yell of excited discovery and plunged his hands into the water.

Arthur sighed. 'I feel sorry for the crabs...'

'Jack, I've got your armbands,' called Molly. 'Don't go in the water without them, OK?'

'I'm not going in the boring old water,' shouted Jack. 'There's *crabs*!'

Arthur rolled his eyes meaningfully. 'See?'

Molly laughed. 'Well, *I'm* going in. Let's see how long it takes him to get jealous.'

Already wearing their swimming things beneath their clothes, Molly and Arthur stripped off their jeans and T-shirts, flung them onto the nearest rocks and raced shrieking into the water. Molly gasped as she splashed deeper, but that was only the first shock – once they were in properly, the water wasn't too cold at all. After a few brisk strokes, she rolled onto her back and floated lazily, gazing up at the crystal blue of the sky. Gulls wheeled and cried, and from further along she could hear the clamour of puffins and kittiwakes on the cliffs. She closed her eyes to feel the warmth of the sun on her eyelids.

Seawater crashed into her face, making her splutter and flip upright. Arthur, laughing, flicked another handful at her.

'Isn't this great?'

Molly laughed and sent a huge splash back in his direction, but Arthur had already dived down, and Molly only soaked her cousin's legs as he executed an elegant underwater handstand.

Just a few weeks ago she might have bristled at her cousin's teasing, Molly thought with a grin, but saving children from nasty Shadowsprye turned out to be a great way to make friends! Well, they'd definitely got over their rocky beginning, but Arthur still deserved a return soaking. And he had to breathe eventually… Molly trod water, waiting with narrowed eyes for her chance of revenge.

Just then, a flicker of distant movement caught her attention. Distracted, Molly frowned at a smudge on the horizon.

'Oi! You haven't surrendered, have you?'

Molly glanced around as Arthur resurfaced. 'Oh, that's so annoying! I could have got you then.'

'Missed your chance.' Her cousin swam idly to her side. 'What is it?'

'There, do you see?' Molly had to shade her eyes. 'It looks like an old-fashioned ship – you know? The ones with tall masts and sails?'

Maybe it was just a trick of the light, though, because the ship was only a smear of shadow – and as the two of them peered, trying to make it out, it vanished. Molly blinked and rubbed her wet face.

'Where did it go?' asked Arthur. 'Back over the horizon?'

'I...suppose so.' Molly was doubtful, but it was the only explanation.

'Hey!' That was Jack, paddling up to his knees in the water and pointing out at the horizon. 'A vanishing ship!'

'Jack!' scolded Molly, swimming back towards him. 'Don't come in any deeper without your armbands.'

'Was that magic? It *disappeared*!'

'It's just an optical illusion.' All the same, Molly felt a little ripple of suspicion pass through her. 'Like what Mum and Dad do on stage.'

'I don't know why anyone would want to magic away a *ship*,' insisted Jack.

'Nobody did—' began Molly, exasperated, but Arthur tapped her on the shoulder and pointed out towards the horizon.

'We'd better get out of the water, Molly.' There was disappointment in her cousin's voice. 'So much for summer!'

Sure enough, the sunlight had dimmed, and there

was a distinctly chilly breeze on Molly's face. She turned in the water to see that the horizon had vanished as completely as the half-seen ship. The familiar Ravenstorm Island mist was rolling in across the sea, a wet gloomy bank of white cloud, and the water was growing choppier. Molly felt a big swell lift her off her feet, then subside. The power of it gave her a nervous flutter in her stomach.

'You're right, Art,' she said dismally, swimming after her cousin against the tug of the withdrawing waves.

Their feet grounded on sand and both of them stumbled out of the sea, Molly seizing Jack's reluctant hand, and they ran for their clothes. Jack was all right – he'd never taken his clothes off, just let his shorts get soaked as he paddled – but Molly and Arthur had to towel themselves down quickly and struggle into sandy jeans and T-shirts, the fabric clinging to them damply.

'Yuck!' shouted Arthur, as huge raindrops began to spatter on them. He grabbed his trainers and ran up the beach, ducking his head into the now-driving rain. Reaching back for Jack's hand, he pulled him up onto the concrete ramp that marked the beginning of Kelp Street. Molly scrambled up behind them, then glanced back at the sea.

How could things change so fast? The weather reminded her uneasily of the mist that had rolled in that day they'd been up on the cliffs, when she and Arthur had lost Jack to the evil-tempered Queen of the Shadowsprye. That fog too had descended without warning. Molly was getting used to the changeable Ravenstorm Island climate, but this was ridiculous.

The sea was roaring now, waves crashing and sucking at the sand, the wind screaming as it tossed and buffeted the gulls like scraps of white rag. Distant thunder crashed, and rain rattled down onto them. There wasn't much point running for cover, Molly realised – they were already soaked through.

'Look, there *is* a boat!' yelled Jack, dragging on Arthur's hand to pull him back round. 'Look!'

'Of course there isn't— Oh!' Molly put her hands to her mouth. 'Art!'

They all stared helplessly as the drenching rain sluiced down. Jack was right – there was no sign of the mysterious high-masted ship, but there was certainly a boat out there in the raging water. A small sailing boat was being tossed helplessly by the gigantic waves, its loose sail flapping wildly and dragging it sideways, even as water crashed across its bows and deck. As they watched, it spun in a half-circle and keeled crazily.

'They're in trouble,' exclaimed Molly. 'Real trouble!'

'We've got to get help!' shouted Arthur. 'It's just a little dinghy!'

'Come on!' yelled Molly over the howl of the wind and the crash of the waves. Seizing Jack's free hand, she helped Arthur pull him away, and then they were all bolting desperately up Kelp Street.

'Where to?' panted Arthur. 'Who should we tell?'

'Whoever's in the first house. Come on!' Molly hauled Jack after her. 'I don't know where the coastguard is, but they will!'

Ahead on their left was a rusting iron gate. Arthur flung it open and ran up the cinder path, Molly at his heels and Jack's small legs pumping desperately to keep up. Molly hoped this house wasn't rented out to tourists – they wouldn't know what to do, and they'd have to look somewhere else, and time would run out, and—

It didn't look like a holiday house, though, she realised, panting for breath. Wind-and-weather-beaten, the little cottage's whitewashed walls were crumbly and its garden was strewn with jetsam from the sea. For a horrible moment Molly thought it might be abandoned, but when Arthur hammered frantically with the squid-shaped door knocker, the door opened almost immediately.

'What on earth?' The young woman in the doorway had short, wild brown hair and her green eyes were startled. 'Come inside, you'll—'

'No!' Molly panted for breath. 'There's a boat – out there! In trouble!'

'Can you phone Sergeant Garland?' begged Arthur. 'Is there a coastguard? Please!'

The young woman didn't panic at all; her face grew grim. 'I can do better than that.'

She turned away, and for an instant Molly feared she was going to slam the door on them and the lashing rain. But instead she grabbed a waterproof jacket from a coat rack behind her, threw a neatly wrapped orange canvas bundle to Molly, and ran out ahead of them, down the path.

'The jetty!' she called over her shoulder, the rain already plastering her brown hair to her head. 'I have a launch. Best chance – and the quickest!'

They pounded after her down Kelp Street, this time following her around to the right instead of jumping down onto the beach. In front of them there was a ramp and a little jetty, its boards wet and alarmingly slippery, but the young woman raced confidently ahead. A motorboat was moored to it, and she jumped down into its open cabin, wasting no time in gunning the engine into life.

Molly and Arthur, much more cautious with Jack in tow, reached the boat as the woman stowed its mooring ropes and it began to draw away from the jetty. They stared down anxiously at her, Jack held firmly between them, and she grinned up and winked.

'Don't worry,' she yelled. 'And I'm Charley, by the way!'

And then Charley and the little boat were slewing away from the jetty in a wake of white foam, curving out across the water and cutting through the waves.

'Where's the other boat?' cried Molly, desperately scanning the wildly choppy sea. 'Is it still there? Art, it's gone.'

'No – there!' Arthur gasped. As the swell rose and subsided, they could see the dinghy once more; at least, they could see its white keel. It had capsized already, a few hundred metres from shore, and two figures in bright lifejackets clung desperately to its hull. The waves crashed across them again, and one of the figures almost lost their grip – until the second reached out and dragged them back.

'Come on, Charley, whoever you are,' muttered Molly. 'You've got to save them.'

Charley was taking great care, though; she'd throttled back the engine and the motorboat was bobbing like a toy in the waves as she very cautiously let it drift towards the lee of the upturned yacht. She tossed a lifebelt towards the pair of stranded sailors; the stronger one grabbed it awkwardly, and then Charley was hauling on the rope.

'Let go of the boat!' they heard her yell over the noise of the storm. 'I'll pull you in. Let go, it's safe!'

Molly held her breath. She didn't think she'd want to leave the safety of that upturned hull, even though it could go under any minute. But the two sailors must have trusted the authority in Charley's voice. The first – the stronger one – released their hold, and the second had to go with them. For long painful minutes they were tossed helplessly in the swell, waves crashing over their heads, but slowly and surely Charley was hauling them in. She'd looped the end of the rope around a cleat on the gunwale, so that even when she had to let go briefly to get a better grip, the sailors were not washed away more than a few feet.

Molly felt Arthur's fingers tight on her arm, and she realised that her cousin was as anxious as she was. But at last the floundering bodies washed closer to Charley's boat, and she dragged them closer still; in seconds they were right against the hull of her little boat. Leaning down, Charley grabbed each in turn beneath the armpits and helped them scramble up a ladder and over the gunwale. When both sailors had slumped to safety on board, Molly couldn't help but jump up and down, cheering.

'Yay!' screamed Jack, beside himself with the thrill of it all. 'Yay, Charley! She rescued them!'

Arthur looked more shakily relieved than overjoyed, but he was grinning and bouncing on his heels. Charley gave them a cheerful wave and yelled something as the motorboat surged back through the churning sea towards them.

Above the howl of the wind and the roar of the engine through the waves, Molly made out the words, 'Guys! Get ready!' She was mystified only a moment, until she remembered the pack Charley had thrown her.

'Let's get this open.' She yanked the straps loose and unrolled the pack, and Arthur helped her draw out two flimsy silver-foil blankets, folded into neat squares.

Arthur shook one out. 'Emergency blankets. Charley's kind of well-prepared, isn't she?'

Molly nodded, curious, but by now Charley was steering the boat against the jetty, where it bumped against a line of old tyres. Her half-drowned passengers were a balding man and a shocked-looking woman with a bedraggled ponytail.

When she flung a rope towards them, Arthur grabbed it and looped it round a bollard while Molly guided the two drenched sailors ashore. Even Jack helped wrap the silver blankets around them both, his face serious for once – and a little self-important, thought Molly with an inward smile.

Charley climbed out of the boat and patted Jack's shoulder proudly. 'Good man!'

'Absolutely.' The woman sailor's teeth were chattering, but she managed to smile at them all. 'Thank you. Thank you *so much*.'

The man nodded, squeezing the woman's shivering body with an arm. 'Yes, thank you. I feel like an idiot. I'm so sorry. But the weather was perfect, and the forecast—'

'That's Ravenstorm Island for you,' said Charley kindly. 'You're visitors here, aren't you?'

'Yes… But it's not our first visit. I should have known better… I'm Michael, by the way.' He held out a dripping, freezing hand. 'This is my wife, Shona…'

Charley laughed. 'Oh please, don't worry about formal introductions. But I'm Charley. And don't worry about misjudging the weather, either. It's so changeable around the island, and we have our own little microclimate. I'm afraid even the best forecasts can be wrong.'

'Even so. I thought we had everything covered, but—'

'That ship.' His wife shuddered. 'It happened *just* when that ship appeared.'

'Shona, we agreed it wasn't—'

'I know. But it's true! As soon as those sails appeared, the storm blew up. Out of nowhere!'

Molly and Arthur exchanged a furtive glance. *The ship*, Molly thought, excitement tingling inside her. The mysterious vanishing ship…

The man was looking apologetically at Charley, who wore a sceptical expression. 'I have to say, it was an incredible coincidence. We'd just remarked on how strange it looked – those old sails, and the rigging.'

'A pirate ship!' yelled Jack. 'We saw it too!'

At Charley's expression of surprise, Molly blushed and shrugged slightly. 'We did. At least, we thought we might have…'

'A tall ship, you mean?' Charley raised an eyebrow.

'They're not so unusual, you know. It could well have been a sail training organisation, or historical marine society...'

'But the sails were all tattered and torn!' exclaimed Shona. 'A training ship wouldn't go out like that. Not unless it wanted to show the pupils some *real* trouble!'

'And then – well.' Michael inhaled deeply, as if gathering his nerve. 'The wind. I know it sounds far-fetched, but the wind came down exactly when that ship appeared.'

'Yes, it did.' Jack nodded fiercely, ignoring Molly's finger at her lips.

'It was as if the ship brought the storm with it! And where did it come from, anyway?' demanded Shona. 'We didn't see it when we sailed out this morning.' It's all very odd!

Charley shook her head firmly. 'I know all the shipping on these waters, and there aren't any tall ships moored here; the harbour isn't big enough. Maybe it sailed from the mainland. But it could just as easily have been a trick of the light, you know. You do get some *very* strange effects out at sea, and you've had a bad shock—'

'*We* didn't get a shock,' insisted Jack stubbornly. 'And *we* saw it.'

'Quiet, Magic Boy,' whispered Arthur. 'We could have been seeing things.'

'Yes, *exactly*! That's what I said! We saw a *ship*!'

Arthur laughed. 'That's not what I meant—'

'No,' Michael interrupted firmly. 'It was definitely a rigged ship, like a schooner maybe – and it sailed pretty close to us. Well, if it was a training vessel, I hope the crew's OK.'

'Oh, my goodness,' exclaimed Shona, slightly shamefaced. 'I hope it didn't get into the same trouble as us. You're right, Charley, of course. It must have been our imagination – about the storm being brought by the ship. You know.' She blushed, seeming to realise quite suddenly how silly it all sounded. 'It was a coincidence, that's all,' she added with a reassuring smile at Jack.

Molly thought Jack seemed more disappointed than comforted.

'Absolutely.' Michael nodded and sighed. 'The sea does do that to you, sometimes. Just a… Well, a trick of the light, as you say.'

Charley rubbed her hands briskly, dismissing the subject. 'If you're feeling a little better, you must come back to my house now – it's only up the hill. You need hot drinks – and I need to call the coastguard and the police about your dinghy. Best if we get you somewhere warm.'

They nodded and rose, still full of thanks for their rescue – they seemed to have dismissed the subject of the mysterious ship.

Molly caught the meaningful glance Arthur shot her. Her cousin looked as if he was just managing to contain his excitement. Michael and Shona's story hadn't seemed nearly so bizarre to the two of them as it had to Charley.

Molly grinned at Arthur. *We're going to have a lot to discuss later…*

Her hand went unthinkingly to the pendant at her throat. The smooth white stone hung on a leather cord, just as Arthur and Jack wore theirs – because Mason the butler, who had given them the stones in the first place, had insisted they wear them around their necks from now on. It wouldn't do, he said, for any of the stones to go missing, or be left behind at the hall by mistake. After all, look what had happened last time...

Well, quite, thought Molly. Jack had carelessly thrown his stone away, and Arthur had left his behind in the human world on the orders of the Shadowsprye – and without those charms to protect them, they'd both been turned into bewitched statues. It had been up to Molly, still protected by her own spellstone, to break the enchantment.

Molly found she was shivering a little as she took Jack's hand and led him back up the slope towards Charley's cottage. With her free hand she turned the stone pendant in her fingers, rubbing her thumb across its weird but elegant engraving of a raven.

The curls and whorls were beautifully carved and inlaid with black enamel, and something about the shape felt comforting and secure. She certainly wouldn't want to be without it if there were ghost ships in the bay.

If some new magic was stirring on Ravenstorm Island, she could only hope the stones would keep them safe...

Charley got to her feet, setting down her mug of tea, and pulled back the curtain in her front room to stare out of the window, examining the coast in both directions. 'The sun's coming out already,' she remarked. 'That's a Ravenstorm Island storm for you!'

The two tourists shook their heads, looking wonderingly out at the weather, and Michael murmured, 'It's unbelievable.'

'Like it never happened!' added Shona.

Apart from their soaking, the pair of them seemed none the worse for wear; all that was hurt, Shona told them with a rueful smile, was their nautical pride. The couple had refused Charley's offer to call the doctor – and they were certainly having none of the air ambulance – so all Charley could do was provide lots of hot tea, a place to dry out their sodden, salty clothing, and a friendly ear for their bewildered tale of the mysterious tall ship. Although they seemed vaguely embarrassed about their 'hallucination', Michael and Shona kept returning to the subject like a dog to a bone. As she sipped her own hot chocolate, Molly glanced at Charley, and could tell she was still resolutely unconvinced. Molly wasn't so sure.

Finally, after more effusive thanks, and a promise to Charley to let her know if their boat was recovered, Michael and Shona rose, made their excuses and left to return to their guesthouse.

'Well,' said Charley, when she and the children were alone. 'More hot chocolate? Or would you rather go back to the beach?'

'The beach!' yelled Jack, before Molly or Arthur could open their mouths.

Arthur shrugged at Charley and smiled. 'I think

I'm probably all full of hot chocolate anyway.'

'Me too,' said Molly. 'Thanks, Charley. I don't know what we'd have done if you hadn't been here.'

'Oh, someone else would have come to the rescue.' Charley smiled as she gathered up their empty cups. 'Ravenstorm Island's good that way.'

'So you're the local lifeboat?' asked Molly. She could hardly believe their luck in running straight to the right house, if that was so.

'Me? Heavens, no! The lifeboat's based on the mainland. But I know the currents around the island as well as anyone, so I didn't think there wasn't any point delaying while we called the lifeboat out.' Her green eyes twinkled.

'But what do you do, then?' asked Arthur, curious.

'I'm a marine biologist. I study wildlife in the waters around the island, so I'd be in trouble if I didn't keep tabs on the sea conditions and the tides. As a matter of fact, I'll come down to the beach with you now. I'd like to take a look at the intertidal zone after that storm.'

'The what?' Jack was gazing at her with adulation.

Charley grinned at him. 'The interesting bit! The area the sea leaves behind when the tide goes out. There's always loads to find and study, Jack. And it gives me a really good idea of the health of the coastal waters.'

It didn't take Charley long to clear away the mugs. She refused to let them wash up – 'It's always chaos in this house; I'll deal with it later,' she told them firmly – so they were soon back at the end of Kelp Street, Jack running eagerly ahead, the sun shining brilliantly again on wet stone and slates and tarmac. As they jumped down onto the sand, Molly saw that the sea was once more calm and welcoming, small waves licking at the sand and flecks of sunlight dancing on the water further out.

'It's amazing how fast the weather changes,' Molly said. She shook her head. 'It was kind of scary being in the sea when that storm blew up.'

'It's usually safe, but you need to stay alert,' Charley told them. 'Don't stray too far from the shore, that's all I can say. The currents are strong – and tricky! That's why the marine life around here is so rich.'

'And that'll explain the mermaids,' said Arthur, deadpan, as he hooked his towel over a rock and began to strip down to his trunks again.

Charley laughed. 'Now that's something I've never found washed up.'

'Give it time,' murmured Arthur under his breath, making Molly choke on a suppressed giggle.

'Oh, there are plenty of interesting creatures in these waters without having to make them up! Tell you what, you won't find any mermaids, but there are lots of mermaids' purses.' Slipping off her shoes and rolling up her trouser legs, Charley stepped confidently up onto a flat shelf of seaweed-covered rock where Jack was already rummaging in a shallow pool. She bent down and lifted a square brown sac, holding it out for Jack's inspection. 'See? It's a case for sharks' eggs!'

'There are *sharks*?' Jack's eyes lit up.

'Not the kind that'll eat you,' laughed Charley;

then, seeing the disappointment in Jack's eyes, she added, 'probably. See these tendrils at the corners? They help fix the case to the seabed. It keeps the eggs safe and secure till they hatch.'

Barefoot, Molly and Arthur clambered up to join Charley and Jack; the barnacles were sharp against their feet and Art almost slithered on the wet weed. Grabbing Molly's arm, he righted himself. 'Look, Charley's a magician too. She's silenced Jack!'

Molly grinned. Sure enough, Jack was staring enchanted into his bucket as Charley picked out his treasures and explained them.

'That's a periwinkle. A little sea snail. It's still alive, so be sure to put it back, OK?' Charley held the tiny shell up to show him. 'There's a little trapdoor, see it there? It keeps the water in when the tide goes out, so the animal inside survives till the sea covers it again.'

'Wow,' breathed Jack. 'But can't I keep it? I'll make sure the bucket stays full of water…'

'No, you can't!' Molly told him firmly, visions

filling her head of Jack's room at Ravenstorm Hall turning into a rather smelly aquarium.

'This zone's a tough place to live,' pointed out Charley, 'what with the tide coming in and out, and the sea crashing in when there's a storm. You wouldn't want to make that little thing's life any harder, would you?'

'Well…' Jack didn't sound at all sure.

'Come on, let's find some old shells,' suggested Molly. 'If they're empty you can have as many as you like.'

'Absolutely,' agreed Charley, with a wink at Molly. 'Let's find some really good specimens. And you can have this mermaid's purse, Jack! The eggs hatched long ago.'

'Ooh! Thanks.' Jack set the little snail carefully back in the rock pool, then followed Charley, Molly and Art as they picked their way across the rocks, hunting for empty shells. There were plenty of those to keep Jack happy, together with a dead crab and even an old sea urchin shell. It was as delicate as porcelain, the spines broken away to leave a nubbly lilac surface.

Wandering a little way from the others, Molly soon found herself at the edge of the long shelf of rock. Beneath it the sea foamed up and retreated to leave puddles of seawater in crannies and hollows.

Molly cautiously picked her way on bare feet along the edge, where the waves surged and caves had been hollowed out of the cliffs. Crouching, she peered over. The tide had dug sizeable hollows in the sand beneath the rock, and as she narrowed her eyes and peered closer, she could see something gleaming there, half-hidden by drifting kelp.

It might be nothing more than an old, half-rusted bit of equipment lost overboard from a fishing boat – a hook, maybe, or a broken cleat? – but Jack seemed fascinated by all the flotsam they'd collected; here was something else she could retrieve to keep him happy. Narrowing her eyes, she gripped the crusty rock with one hand and let herself carefully down into the water, as a wave rushed in around her knees.

The sand was churned up at her feet, and she had to bend to rummage in the swirling murk, pebbles knocking into her shins. Though the sea was much calmer now, its force and tug were still quite alarming. Molly had lost sight of the gleaming object, and for a moment she thought the thing had been sucked back out again by the tide; then her fingers closed around something hard and heavy beneath the strands of kelp. Tugging it from its sandy bed, she stood up and turned it in her hands, water streaming off it. Molly wiped off as much sand and grit as she could, and peered closer.

It was no plain scrap of discarded machinery, but an old compass, big enough that she had to hold it in both hands to examine it properly. The metal case was dull from lying in the seawater, and the dome of glass was scratched, but when she picked off the last strands of weed she could see that the compass's face was beautifully engraved and painted, with pictures of a smiling sun and a glowering crescent moon, and fierce-looking cherubs blowing wind from east and west. Sixteen points of the compass were inscribed in an elaborate flowing script.

'What have you found, Molly?' Arthur was looking down from the rocky shelf, Charley at his side. 'I was about to send Charley out to sea to rescue you.'

Molly reached up a hand and let Art pull her back onto the barnacle-crusted outcrop. 'Look at this. Someone must have lost it off a boat, I think!' She chewed her lip as she turned the compass in her hands. It was a very beautiful thing – could it be a real antique? Surely not... She shook her head slowly. 'I think it's maybe a souvenir. Quite a good one. Do they sell these on the island?'

Charley took the compass from her hands and studied it, impressed. 'I've never seen anything like this in the gift shop on Kelp Street. It doesn't look like a modern souvenir to me. It looks old.'

'Really old,' agreed Arthur, touching a cautious fingertip to the glass. The pointer quivered and crept round to the north. 'And it's still working. I bet my mum and dad would like to see it. They're antiques dealers,' he added for Charley's benefit.

Jack had joined them now, straining to peer at the compass, and Charley held it lower for him to study. 'Your parents must be the Wolfreys, then? The people who just bought Ravenstorm Hall?'

'That's them. They *love* old stuff.'

'I expect they'll be able to tell you more, then. It's a fascinating thing, isn't it?' Charley stroked the scratched glass. 'Let me know what they say!'

Since Jack's bucket was full of shells and pebbles by now, and he'd topped it up to the brim with seawater, they set off back across the beach, taking turns to hold and examine Molly's find. When they reached their pile of belongings, Molly stowed the compass safely in her beach bag, wrapped in a towel, before they pulled their clothes back on again.

'We didn't get to have another swim,' pointed out Arthur, tugging his T-shirt over his head. 'Let's come back tomorrow, if the weather's better. It's well worth it to keep Magic Boy happy.'

They waved goodbye to Charley at her garden

gate and headed for the road to Ravenstorm Hall, with Jack clutching his bucket possessively against his chest; Molly didn't think she'd ever seen him take so much care with anything. But no sooner had they taken a few steps up Kelp Street than a cool breeze ran across Molly's skin, raising goosebumps on her arms. She glanced up at the darkening sky. The sun was first reduced to a pale disc, then blotted out altogether by gathering black heaps of cumulus cloud.

'Oh no,' she moaned. 'We're going to get soaked again!'

'Run!' said Arthur as the first huge raindrops spattered their heads.

Molly seized Jack's hand and raced after her cousin. Driving rain lashed their faces, but Jack didn't loosen his tight grip on the bucket handle. By the time they reached the lane that led to Ravenstorm Hall, and were slightly sheltered by overhanging beeches, they were already drenched to the skin. Panting, Molly slowed to a brisk walk.

'We're soaked already,' she yelled above the racket of the downpour. 'We might as well save our breath and walk!'

Jack, his blond hair plastered to his forehead, shook his hand loose from hers and peered into his bucket with some satisfaction. 'My ocean's going to overflow! Wonder if I can make a tidal wave.'

'This weather's unbelievable, even for Ravenstorm Island,' grumbled Arthur. 'Look at the ravens! They aren't happy.'

Ahead, they could see the turrets of Ravenstorm Hall, black and forbidding against the granite sky. Lightning crackled beyond it, and once again the ravens that nested in the trees had taken to the skies, wheeling and cawing.

'You'd think they'd have the sense to stay among the branches,' remarked Molly. 'I know I would! Come on, Jack, we're nearly home.'

The great gates were just ahead, their stone posts dark and sodden, the wrought iron dripping. Molly broke into a run again, guiding Jack with an arm round his shoulders – but as they shoved the gates ajar and jogged between the posts, a massive shape loomed abruptly from the shadows.

Molly couldn't help but gasp and skid to a halt, making Arthur stumble into her and almost knock her over. Her shock faded quickly to relief, though, as she smiled up at the grim figure of Mason.

His craggy features shifted into something like a smile as he held out an enormous black umbrella. It was so huge it gave all three of them some shelter against the downpour.

'Come along, I thought all of you might be getting drenched.'

Molly cuddled Jack close as they hurried up the drive under the umbrella. 'Hold it higher, Mason, and you'll keep dry too.'

'I don't think so, Molly. Besides, I'm quite used to getting wet.' He gave her a solemn sidelong wink.

That was true, she supposed. No doubt he was often soaked up there on the roof of the hall with the other gargoyles.

'Thanks, Mason!' Arthur darted up the steps as they reached them, Molly and Jack at his heels. Ponderous as ever, Mason furled the umbrella as he climbed after them.

'Off you go to the kitchen,' he told the children, closing the great oak door against the driving torrent and ushering them across the vast hall. 'The stove's lit, and it's warm. We'll soon get you dry, and I daresay I can find some hot chocolate somewhere.'

'I know you will,' said Arthur, pushing open the kitchen door. 'You're the best, Mason. Come on, Jack, take those shoes off before your feet dissolve completely.'

Looking quite alarmed, Jack rapidly toed off his little trainers and bent to check his feet were still there, before casting Arthur a scowl. 'They're not even dissolved a bit.'

'Phew! Just in time, Magic Boy. Pale and wrinkly, but still in place. Oi, where are you going now?'

Jack grinned as he heaved his sloshing bucket towards Aunt Catherine's study. 'I'm going to show

Aunt Cathy and Uncle Bill my ocean!'

Molly was about to grab him when Arthur tugged her sleeve. 'Let him go. Mum adores him, and it'll keep him out of our hair for five minutes.'

'And it'll give me time to get the chocolate made,' added Mason, 'without a certain young man licking his finger and dipping it in the cocoa canister.'

Molly grinned, and tipped the sodden contents of her beach bag onto the huge wooden table. 'We might even get this stuff dry, if we hang it over the stove. Oh!'

She'd almost forgotten her beachcombing find, until something large and heavy thudded and rolled out of the crumpled towel. Molly made a wild grab for the compass before it could roll off the table, and let out a breath of relief when it clattered to stillness beneath her hand.

'Phew! That was close. Mason, see what we—'

But as she glanced up, she fell silent. The butler's greyish skin had gone a deathly shade of white. She had never seen him look even remotely surprised before; now his mouth opened in shock and his eyes were wide and horrified as he stared at the compass.

'Mason?' Arthur nudged his arm lightly. 'What's wrong?'

He didn't reply, just reached out a trembling hand and touched the compass's glass face.

He looks like he's afraid it'll give him an electric shock or something, Molly thought.

His fingers clenched and unclenched, and he made himself lift the compass. Slowly he turned it, swallowing hard as he studied the delicate engraving on its face. Though it had seemed so dull and tarnished from its time in the seawater, glinting light now reflected off the glass and onto Mason's face, making him blink against the brightness.

'Where did you find this?' His voice sounded even more gravelly than usual.

Molly frowned, still watching his expression. 'On the beach. It must have washed up – oh, off a ship, I guess.'

'Off a ship,' he echoed hoarsely. 'Did you – did you see the ship?'

'No…' Arthur tilted his head, curious. 'Why?'

'No – no reason.' He cleared his throat, then coughed into his fist.

Molly caught Arthur's eye. *A ship!*

'We were saying that it looks like an antique,' Molly remarked pointedly. 'It's likely it came off quite an *old* ship.' Eyeing him closely, she prodded, 'What do you think, Mason?'

'I – yes, you're probably right. I'll – get the milk boiled, shall I…?'

'Because we actually *did* see an old ship. Earlier today,' Molly added. 'Didn't we, Arthur?'

'Yes, we did.' Arthur narrowed his eyes at Mason. 'A tall ship. The *old-fashioned* kind. You don't think it could have sunk in the storm?'

'Tall ship,' echoed Mason again, faintly.

'Yes.' Molly folded her arms. 'One of those old-style sailing ships, with rigging and masts and everything. We saw it this morning, before the storm broke. I'm not sure it would be strong enough to withstand this weather. We're a bit worried.'

'No need. Not at all,' he announced, too loudly. 'Old ships are very...resilient. Sturdily, uh...built.'

Arthur, too, was watching Mason suspiciously. 'But it vanished. Just vanished!'

'Trick of the light.' Mason cleared his throat loudly. 'I should have thought you'd know all about those, Molly, what with your parents being famous magicians.' He turned away and bustled overenthusiastically at the stove.

Trick of the light. Just what Charley had called the ship! Only Mason sounded lot less like he believed it than Charley had...

'Mason, *are* there tall ships in these waters? Charley said there weren't.'

'Charley? Oh, yes. Starfish Cottage on Kelp Street. A dear young lady. Always helpful.'

'Yes. And she rescued a couple from their capsized dinghy this morning.' Arthur glared at Mason's broad back. '*They* saw the ship too.'

'As a matter of fact,' added Molly, 'they thought the ship caused the storm.'

'Nonsense.' They couldn't see Mason's face now, but his guffaw sounded forced. 'Tourists do imagine things on this island. They aren't used to the, er…the strange climate. I told you, it was a trick of the light.'

Molly dared to edge a little closer to him as she raised her eyebrows at Arthur. 'Mason, did the compass upset you? I'm sorry if I—'

'Good heavens, child. Don't be silly. I'm not fond of storms, that's all. It comes of living so close to the sea.' He stepped back from the stove. 'Here. The milk's almost boiled and the chocolate's right there. I've got rather a lot to do around the hall, so if you'll excuse me?'

And he strode, huge fists clenched, from the kitchen.

As the door clunked shut behind him, Arthur and Molly stared at each other.

'Well, *that* was weird,' said Arthur. 'Yet again.'

Molly shrugged. 'He's always a bit funny, but that

compass definitely upset him.' She touched it with the tip of her forefinger, suddenly nervous. 'As for him being frightened by storms – that's nonsense! The first night I came here he was wandering around on the roof in the thunder and lightning!'

'There's something he's not telling us.' Arthur scooped chocolate powder into three mugs and poured over the hot milk, his lips pursed thoughtfully. 'And that makes me think something's up. You know, I think I won't show that compass to my parents – not quite yet. Let's wait until we know a bit more. Because I'm sure there's more to find out.'

'Yes.' Molly grinned. 'This being Ravenstorm Island and all.'

'Exactly!' Arthur pushed a steaming mug across the table towards her. 'If there's something magical happening – and we know Mason's part of all that – then I don't want to have to start explaining it to my parents.'

'Ugh, no. They'll certainly never believe a story about a magical compass!'

'What's more, they never did find out about the Shadowsprye, and the child statues.' Arthur blew on the surface of his drink. 'And I'm not about to start telling them now…'

For now, keeping the compass from Arthur's parents was definitely the best strategy, Molly reflected later that night. There were some truths, she was certain, that adults simply couldn't handle.

She, Art and Jack were gathered with Art's parents around the drawing room's roaring fire, listening to the storm rage and beat against the windows. Sometimes there was nothing nicer than huddling cosily indoors, safe and warm, while the weather howled and screamed outside.

Besides, Aunt Catherine seemed distracted and anxious enough without them telling her fairytales. She'd just come back for the umpteenth time from baby Harriet's room, pushing strands of brown hair out of her tired eyes.

'She won't settle at all,' she told Uncle Bill,

gratefully taking the mug of tea he offered and clasping her hands tightly around it. 'I hope she's not getting sick.'

'She's a bit out of sorts, that's all,' her husband reassured her. 'Let her calm herself for a bit. I'm sure she'll fall asleep soon.'

'I'll give it five minutes, then.' Aunt Catherine sank wearily into an armchair.

Molly jumped up, feeling guilty that she and Jack were causing extra work for Arthur's parents just when they'd only recently had a new baby. 'I'll go and make more tea,' she offered. 'A fresh pot will taste better.'

Uncle Bill gave her a grateful look as she headed for the kitchen.

I hope Harriet goes to sleep before I get back, she thought. *Poor Aunt Catherine!*

She felt quite at home in the big kitchen, she realised happily as she set the kettle on the stove to boil. Making friends with Arthur had made a huge difference, after all their mutual hostility at the beginning. And so long as Jack didn't get into any more trouble – like being turned into a statue, Molly thought with a fond roll of her eyes – she knew they'd be very happy here for the summer. In some ways she longed for the island's magic to show itself again; but it would be awful for Aunt Catherine to have any more to worry about. *Just a small extra adventure would be fine,* she thought: *something not too dangerous…*

Leaning against the worktop as she waited for the kettle to whistle, she eyed Jack's bucket. He'd set it down next to the sink, still full of shells and stones, but water had slopped over the sides and was dripping onto the wooden floor.

Oh, no, Jack; that was careless. And Aunt Catherine and Uncle Bill were very particular, she knew, about keeping the hall neat and tidy.

Molly tore off a piece of kitchen towel to mop it up, but when she went to the bucket, she gasped and crumpled up the towel in her fist.

Jack's miniature ocean was whipped up into its

very own storm. Tiny waves surged and crashed, flinging up spray and swamping over the edge of the bucket. Molly took a shocked step back, then crept closer and peered in again. A wave splashed up into her face, shockingly cold.

Molly shook her head and wiped her eyes. *The wind must be blowing into the kitchen*, she thought wildly. *It must be hitting the bucket dead on...* She hurried to close whichever window had banged open – but no. Leaning on the worktop, Molly stared around in confusion. Every single window was firmly shut and bolted against the weather.

This was crazy. Was there something alive in Jack's bucket, despite all Charley's warnings: something that was big enough to struggle? Molly risked sliding her fingers inside and rummaging gently among the pebbles and shells, but all she got was a wet arm and another faceful of spray. She laid a tentative hand on the worktop – perhaps the dishwasher was running and shaking the floor under the bucket – but the surface didn't vibrate at all. The pipes, then

– the ancient clanking plumbing of the hall? But Molly quickly dismissed that idea. No drainage system, however dodgy, could shake a whole enormous kitchen!

Yet still the miniature storm raged in Jack's bucket of seawater.

A thrill ran across her shoulder blades. Magic? It had to be… And was it something to do with that ghostly vanishing ship? If it had somehow stirred up the storm earlier, perhaps it was close by now, and affecting even a little boy's pretend ocean?

The kettle whistled shrilly, startling Molly out of her unnerving thoughts. Swiftly making up a fresh pot of tea, she carried it back through to the drawing room. The heavy curtains were drawn, but she could hear the lash of rain against the windows beyond, and the howling of a gale in the chimney. The flames in the hearth danced and gushed and flared again.

'Oh, thank you Molly! That was kind.' Aunt Catherine reached for the teapot as Molly stared meaningfully at Arthur.

She longed to tell her cousin what had just happened, but Arthur didn't catch her eye. Instead he was winking in a reassuring way at Jack, so Molly sighed and settled down with an arm around her little brother. Telling Arthur would have to wait.

'I'm not scared of storms,' Jack was telling Uncle Bill. 'There was a *huge* one today and I wasn't frightened at all.'

'Good man,' declared Uncle Bill. 'You can hold my hand when I get scared.'

At just that moment, lightning crackled and thunder exploded right outside, shaking the glass panes. Jack started and gasped, and his shoulders tensed beneath Molly's arm. He wasn't quite as cool about the storm as he was pretending, she decided; perhaps he did need a distraction after all. Perhaps they all did. She glanced at the fire as she gave Jack a comforting squeeze.

'I've got an idea. Do you have any card, Art? And scissors and tape?'

Arthur raised an eyebrow. 'I'm sure we do. Why?'

'You'll see in a bit. Oh, and some straws, too, if you've got any.'

'Well, that sounds intriguing.' Arthur's eyes gleamed as he stood up. 'Just give me a moment. I'll have a rake around.'

He was gone for several minutes, while they sat in silence and listened to the battering of the storm, but at last Arthur came back into the library with a sheaf of coloured card and some scissors, and a carton of straws tucked under his arm.

'What are you making, Molly?' asked Uncle Bill curiously.

'I'll show you when I'm finished.' Molly set to work with her materials as the others watched, fascinated. Carefully she clipped shapes out of the card and stuck them to the plastic straws, until she had a little pile of cardboard puppets.

'Oh, that's clever,' said Arthur, picking one up to admire it. 'Here, Dad, look!'

'Molly, that's brilliant! It's a pirate, right?'

'Yes,' said Molly, blushing with pleasure. 'Now if

you put all the lights out, I'll show you one of my dad's party pieces. You like this one, Jack!'

'Oh I know! I *love* this trick!' Jack's eyes gleamed. 'Are you—'

She put a finger to her lips. 'Shh. Don't give the game away, Jack!' Settling before the fire, she winked solemnly at him. 'OK, everybody – watch the wall there, opposite the fire.'

In the darkness, as the light of the flames flickered against the wall, Molly picked up her shadow puppets, cleared her throat and began her story.

'Once,' she told them in her scariest stage-voice, 'there was a ship of savage pirates that roamed the seven seas, forever lost.'

'For*ever* lost?' put in Jack sceptically.

'Shh, Magic Boy!' said Arthur.

'Yes, forever,' Molly told him, lifting the pirate captain she'd shaped with a roaring mouth and narrowed, angry eyes. 'Because it was a – a cursed ship! Doomed to sail to the ends of the earth until they, ah…'

'Found the dragon's treasure!' yelled Jack.

'That'll do nicely,' agreed Molly. 'Yes, the dragon's treasure.' Her sea serpent would do for that, she thought, taking the puppet in her fingers and making its shadow dance threateningly in the flames. 'The dragon that once *bit off the pirate captain's leg*.' Quickly she tore off a paper leg and made the serpent eat its shadow, as Aunt Catherine smiled and relaxed against Uncle Bill's shoulder. Jack was sitting on Arthur's lap, arms round his neck, fascinated by the new variation on the story.

Molly picked up her newest cut-out creation, and Arthur gave a stifled laugh of recognition as a menacing shadow stalked onstage, tall and slender and wearing an elaborate crown and a cape of wings.

'But the pirate captain's ship was bewitched. He'd kidnapped the beautiful daughter of a wicked magical queen, and the queen had turned his crew into fearsome *living statues*…'

* * *

She'd been terribly tempted, Molly mused as she brushed her teeth before bed, to bring a living gargoyle into her pirate story – but she was rather glad she hadn't. Mason might have heard, and been even more upset; and the tale of Captain Boneleg and his crew of enchanted statues had been a great success just as she'd told it.

Poor Mason, she thought. *I wonder what unnerved him so much about the old compass?* She was almost unbearably curious about his reaction, but really, there was no way of bringing it up again tactfully. She and Arthur would just have to wait and see…

Her cousin's eyes had lit up with excitement when Molly at last had a chance to tell him, in a whisper, about the storm in Jack's plastic bucket – but by the time they were able to go to the kitchen to investigate, the bucket and its contents had vanished, probably into Jack's bedroom. All three children were in separate rooms, now that Aunt Catherine had had time to make more of the house habitable, and Molly didn't fancy risking waking Jack up at this hour.

She'd never get her excitable brother back to sleep in this storm.

The rain seemed to have lessened just a little; it no longer hammered so noisily against the glass. Molly leaned forward to the window and pulled aside the blind with a finger. Yes, it was actually possible to see more than a few metres into the night.

She craned her head to peer up at the row of gargoyles on the roof; from here she could just see the empty space at the end, where a figure was missing. So Mason was away from his perch again. Molly squinted out at the grounds, though she doubted he'd be out in the storm. Who would voluntarily go out in that?

Distantly, and out to sea, lightning flashed in the clouds, and Molly gasped. The brief white flare showed a figure on the drive: a familiar, solid, slightly hunched shape. Mason was standing perfectly still, gazing at Ravenstorm Hall.

Darkness shrouded the scene once more, and Molly let the blind fall gently back across the window. A small thrill tickled the nape of her neck.

So Mason was patrolling the grounds again, regardless of the weather. Molly couldn't help but feel as if he was watching them all, protecting them, *guarding* them.

But it wasn't his silent presence that gave her that shiver of fear. What, she wondered uneasily, might he be guarding them against?

Sunshine filled the kitchen the next morning, the blue sky so warm and bright it was as if the terrible storm had been nothing but a dark dream. Molly yawned sleepily as she sat down in her place at the breakfast table. Last night's weather had been real enough, all right. She doubted any of them had slept well, with the crash and roar of the rain and thunder coming and going all night. Aunt Catherine and Uncle Bill looked weary, with dark circles around their eyes.

Arthur had Harriet cradled on his lap, and he was tickling her toes and murmuring animatedly to her – not something Molly could have imagined him doing when they'd first met. But although the baby usually loved Arthur's attention, this morning she just lay there apathetically, her eyes blank and uninterested.

Aunt Catherine gazed anxiously at Harriet over the rim of her coffee cup. 'I really don't think she's well, Bill.'

'She's a little off-colour, that's all.' Uncle Bill patted Catherine's hand. 'Maybe she's colicky?'

'It's not like that at all.' Aunt Catherine took her hand away, pushed it through her hair and sighed. 'She's just listless. I'll have to take her to the doctor if she doesn't improve.'

'I'm sure you won't have to. It's a bug or something. She'll get over it.' But beneath his reassurance, Molly noticed that Uncle Bill looked as worried as his wife. 'You could ask Doctor Barnard if you see him in the village later. He'll know if there's something that ought to be looked at. He's so helpful, even out of hours.'

Molly caught Arthur's eye across the table. Her

cousin looked pale and concerned too. Arthur bent to blow a raspberry on Harriet's tummy, something that usually made her wriggle and kick her chubby legs, but this morning the baby just rolled her head to gaze emptily at her big brother.

'Let's go out after breakfast,' suggested Molly, determined to cheer up Arthur. 'We don't even have to take Jack – he's all wrapped up in his shells and his dead crab.'

The little boy had already dashed away from the breakfast table – after his usual three bowls of Coco Pops – to get back to the undersea kingdom he was creating on the expensive rug in his bedroom.

'That sounds like a good idea.' Uncle Bill slapped his hands together, and winked gratefully at Molly. 'What do you say, Art?'

Arthur nodded, at first a little reluctantly, then with more enthusiasm. 'Yes. OK, Molly.'

'Dad's right. There's no point all three of us moping.' Aunt Catherine smiled at him. 'Go on out with Molly. It's such a beautiful day, you shouldn't waste it. You never know how long it's going to last around here.'

Passing Harriet gently to his father, Arthur kicked back his chair and got to his feet. 'So where will we go?'

'Remember the mist!' called Uncle Bill as they left the kitchen.

'Of course, Dad!' Arthur called back, then grinned at Molly and whispered, 'We've learned our lesson about that, at least. Go on, what do you want to do that doesn't involve going near that cliff?'

Molly thought for a moment. 'I've got an idea. Why don't we go and see Miss Badcrumble? She's got that island museum, and she obviously knows a lot about local history. We could take her the compass, see what she thinks of it? She might even recognise the design.'

'Now, that's a good idea. I certainly wouldn't want to ask Mason again.' Arthur shuddered. 'Besides, we haven't seen Miss B for a while. I miss the nice old weirdo.'

Molly laughed.

It didn't take them long to gather their shoes and emergency rain jackets, and then collect the compass, wrapped up in a towel in Molly's room. Molly folded it carefully into her small backpack and they set off from Ravenstorm Hall, breathing quiet sighs of relief that they didn't bump into Mason, as they often did, on the way out. It was Jack whose running footsteps pursued them to the great front door.

'Hey! Where are you going? I want to come!'

Molly sighed and turned. 'I thought you were playing? We're only going… ah…'

'To the shops,' Arthur filled in. 'For groceries. We're not going anywhere *near* the ice cream parlour, either.'

'Is that all? You're sure?' Jack's face fell.

'Definitely.' Molly crossed her fingers behind her back. 'And we won't be long.'

After all, the last time Jack had been involved in a supernatural adventure, he'd been turned to stone.

Molly really didn't want to risk anything like that happening again.

'All right.' Jack shrugged and went back the way he'd come. 'I'm building Atlantis, anyway. Uncle Bill says it was an ancient lost city under the sea.'

'Uh-huh. And Jack's probably building it so he can flood it all over again,' muttered Arthur under his breath as they closed the door with a clunk and set off down the drive. 'You really think Miss B might know something about the compass?'

Molly shrugged. 'She does know a lot about this island, and all the odd goings-on. And she is a Sprye!'

'One who's lived with humans all her life, though. There's no guarantee she'll know anything about strange compasses or disappearing ships.'

Miss Badcrumble had told them how she'd been brought up by a human family, which had made her grow far beyond the usual height of a Shadowsprye, though she'd been left with the inconvenient birdlike toes and fingers that she had to hide under long skirts and woollen gloves.

'It's worth a try, though.' *Anyway, I really just wanted to get you out of the house, and stop you worrying about Harriet.*

The smell of the sea on the breeze was delicious, and it seemed especially strong this morning. Gulls cried mournfully overhead, riding air currents. Molly couldn't help thinking they looked a little tattered and shellshocked from the wind and rain. She shook her head, grinning. That was probably her imagination.

But when they turned out of the lane into the village of Crowsnest, she wasn't so sure. The two cousins came to an abrupt halt, staring around at a scene of total chaos.

A gigantic beech tree had crashed down right across Main Street; men were around it already, wielding chainsaws, but the road was blocked and warning signs had been set up. Broken slates littered the pavement and gardens, along with leaves and twigs and a smashed 'For Sale' sign. The window of the post office had been hastily blocked with wooden planks, and shards of glass glittered on the ground in the sunshine.

'What on earth?' exclaimed Arthur.

'It must have been the storm.' Molly gazed around in horrified awe. 'But Ravenstorm Hall wasn't touched – you'd think we'd have lost a few slates off the roof, at least, if all this happened here!'

'But the hall hasn't been damaged at all,' agreed Arthur. 'That's just plain…' He searched for a different word, and failed. '*Weird*.'

'Ravenstorm-Island-weird.' Molly nodded. 'Let's go and see if Charley's OK. She's so close to the sea. I hope she hasn't had too much damage.'

As soon as they turned the corner into Kelp Street, Molly gave a cry of horror. Down at the bottom of the road, where the tarmac and cobbles became the concrete ramp that led down to the beach, the usual view was obliterated altogether. A boat had been smashed against the shore by the waves, blocking out the sea. It sagged against the rocks, its cabin windows shattered and its prow splintered.

Molly pointed, aghast. 'That's not Charley's boat, is it?'

Arthur shook his head. 'No, Charley's is smaller and the hull's blue. And look – that must be the crew, over there on the sea wall. But wow, what a mess. Come on!'

The cousins ran down towards the wreckage, but there were plenty of islanders there already, handing out blankets, tea and sympathy to the shocked crew. A few people were clambering round the broken boat, exchanging pessimistic suggestions; others were already dragging bits of smashed fibreglass and wood into a pile by the sea wall.

One of them was a brown-haired young woman in a wetsuit. She glanced round and smiled wearily as Molly and Arthur ran up to her.

'Charley! What happened?'

'It's a mess, isn't it? Those three guys were lucky they got out alive.' She nodded at the pale and shaken crew members.

'We'd no idea the storm was this bad.' Arthur

shook his head. 'It must have been less severe up at the hall.'

'And it was pretty bad there,' added Molly. 'But we didn't have any damage at all.'

'That's extraordinary. Not a tree down or anything? Have you seen Main Street?'

Molly nodded. 'It's a disaster zone.' She turned to the wrecked boat, her hair blustering in the stiff breeze. 'They must have been close to shore…'

'They'd just left the harbour,' said Charley grimly. 'They were heading for their home port on the mainland, because the weather had cleared and the forecast was calm. I didn't even think anything of it – they're local and they know the waters. I saw them motoring out and thought they'd be fine.'

'We thought the storm had passed, too,' said Molly. 'It got quiet about midnight, then nearly blew in my window at two o'clock! The bang woke me up.'

'Out of nowhere,' agreed Charley. 'That's what happened again at six this morning – it lulled us into a false sense of security, then came back with a wallop. Those guys didn't stand a chance when the big wave hit them.'

Arthur grabbed a torn sheet of fibreglass and helped Charley haul it to the pile. 'I'm amazed anybody sails off Ravenstorm Island, if it's this unpredictable,' he said dryly.

'But it isn't!' Slapping her hands together, Charley stepped back, eyeing the wreckage. 'It can be temperamental, that's for sure. But no matter what I told those tourists yesterday, taking a boat out from Ravenstorm Island is usually quite safe. We even let kids your age go out without an adult, as long as they stay in sight of the shore – normally people are only in danger of getting rained on! The forecasts aren't usually *this* unreliable. The last couple of days it's been impossible for the meteorologists to predict anything. They've been blindsided. Even the fishermen were hesitant about going out today, and some of them haven't. There's a shipping warning for the area.'

'At least you've got the lighthouse out on the

cliff,' said Molly, remembering the place where they'd finally tracked down the Queen of the Shadowsprye's lost son Thorn. 'That should keep visiting boats clear.'

'That's the thing, though. We haven't got the lighthouse. It's out of use. Has been for ages – isn't that right, Archie?'

Her last remark was addressed to a bearded man in waterproofs who was dejectedly pushing the wreck's snapped-off prow with a foot.

'Aye,' he said. He took off his hat and scratched his scalp. 'That light's not worked in a hundred years, and there isn't an engineer or an electrician or a flaming sorcerer who can fix it.'

Arthur and Molly exchanged apprehensive glances as Charley laughed.

'Aye, you might laugh, Charlotte Beaumont, but I'm telling the truth. The old fella up at the hall back then, he reckoned himself for a bit of a wizard. Told the islanders in 1922 he'd make the light shine again. When neither they nor it would listen to him, he shut himself in a room up at Ravenstorm Hall and didn't come out for a month. Sulking, see.' A grin flashed across Archie's sullen face. 'That's magicians for you.'

'Well, Molly's parents are magicians.' Art smiled. 'Maybe they should have a go!'

'Good luck to them with that,' muttered Archie gruffly. 'There's a proper old-fashioned curse on that lighthouse, that's what it is.' He clambered away around the boat's prow to inspect the far side of the hull.

Charley shrugged. 'Maybe it is a curse,' she said lightly. 'I went for my usual early-morning dive today, and there's nothing living within five hundred yards of the shore.'

Molly did a double-take. 'Nothing? At all?'

'Barring the kelp, and the molluscs that are stuck to the rocks – and they were all closed up for business. The waters round here are usually teeming!'

Molly shivered suddenly, remembering the miniature storm that had raged in Jack's bucket last night. 'You think it might really be a curse?'

Charley laughed again. 'I think it might be some very smart fish! I reckon they sensed the sea being whipped up and left before the storm arrived. They'll be back. And don't you two take any notice of Archie and his chatter – the weather will go back to normal and so will the sea. It always does.'

'She's right, Molly.' Arthur threw her a meaningful look. 'Listen, we said we'd look in on Miss Badcrumble, remember?'

'Oh, yes!' Molly's hand went to her little backpack, and she swung it up onto her shoulder. 'Come on, then, Art.'

'Oh, she's a sweetie – eccentric but lovely.' Charley turned back to her work. 'Say hello from me.'

'Will do!' Molly gave her a wave as they made their way back through the littered flotsam and jetsam and up onto Kelp Street. 'Arthur,' she said in a low voice, when they were far from the islanders, 'don't you think there has to be something magic about this?'

'I do.' Arthur nodded. 'But Charley wouldn't ever believe it, any more than my mum or dad would.

She's a proper scientist – she'll think it's a load of old superstition. There's only one person who'll take it seriously, and that's our friendly local Shadowsprye!'

If Molly hadn't seen it before, she'd have thought Miss Badcrumble's museum and teashop had sustained some serious storm damage; the building was ancient and crumbling, and its roofline sagged in the middle. But it always looked like that, and a few leaves torn from the shrubbery were the only real sign that the storm had passed. The old plank door stood open, so they knocked and walked in.

'Miss B?' called Arthur.

'Oh!' The voice came from beyond the teashop, in the depths of the museum area. 'I'm in here. Just a moment…'

There was an alarming clatter and bang, and with a troubled glance at one another, Molly and Arthur hurried through into the dimness of the museum. Miss Badcrumble stood balanced at the top of a rickety stepladder, a chaotically crammed shelf at nose-level in front of her. Her long skirt was caught between two rungs, and she had a Tupperware box tucked awkwardly between neck and chin as she fumbled with her gloves. The tattered woollen fingers were, as usual, far too long, and she was struggling to fit them over her hands, but when she caught sight of Molly and Arthur she puffed out a sigh of relief, clutched her rattling box of rocks before it could fall, and blew her straggling hair off her face.

'Oh, it's you!' She gave up the unequal struggle with the gloves and plonked the plastic box onto the last space on the shelf; Molly and Arthur knew all about the three long birdlike talons that the old woman had instead of normal fingers, so there was nothing to hide. Her eyes brightened. 'How nice of you to visit. Cake? Would you like to have some cake?'

'Thanks, Miss B, that would be great.' Arthur fiddled and tugged with the ragged swirling skirt until it was free of the stepladder and Miss Badcrumble could descend in relative safety – though Molly still hovered nervously below, in case she suddenly had to catch the old Sprye as she tumbled.

'Is that a new display?' she asked, curious.

'Yes! Do you like it? Fossils and – things,' the old woman said vaguely, waving a hand up at the new shelf.

Molly squinted up at it, doubtful. One of the fossils up there was rather large, and even in the dim light she could see what looked like the imprints of sharp teeth in the sandstone. *Just a big lizard*, she told herself firmly. *Maybe a dinosaur – certainly not a dragon…*

Miss Badcrumble seemed pleased to have visitors, and she bustled around the teashop until she had assembled a tray with a teapot, mugs and three kinds of cake. 'Now, what's been going on here on the island? I've been ever so busy, and I haven't heard a single scrap of news.'

'Your garden survived the storm last night,' said Arthur. 'That's good.'

'Storm? Oh, my. Oh dear. I suppose there's a terrible lot of damage in the village?'

Arthur rolled his eyes and grinned at Molly. 'Yes, quite a big storm, Miss B.'

'I thought you both looked a little worried.' Miss Badcrumble bit into a slice of seed cake.

'Well… That isn't just the storm,' confessed Molly. 'There's something else we wanted to talk to you about.' She hesitated, remembering Mason's reaction. What if Miss Badcrumble was just as shocked?

Arthur broke in. 'Yes. Molly found something unusual on the beach yesterday, Miss B, and we thought you might be able to tell us about it.'

'Oh?' Miss Badcrumble leaned forward eagerly, scattering crumbs, as Molly rummaged in her backpack. At last her fingers closed on the compass, and she drew it out and set it on the table between them.

The old Sprye gazed at it, perplexed, but showed no sign of shock or horror. 'It's very pretty. And you found it in the sea, you say? Oh dear. I expect someone was very sorry to lose that.'

'It's lovely, isn't it?' Molly stroked the glass casing, relieved. 'But we've no idea how to start finding out where it came from. We thought you might know something about it? After all, you know such a lot about local history.'

Miss Badcrumble looked flattered, but she shook her head dolefully. 'I'm afraid not, dears. I've never seen anything like this.'

'Oh.' Molly was deflated.

Miss Badcrumble brightened again. 'Have you asked Mason? He's been on this island even longer than I have, he might know something about it.'

'That's just it,' said Arthur. 'When we showed it to him, I thought he was going to faint with shock. I daren't ask again in case he has a heart attack.'

'Oh, dear me, no. No, of course not. That's thoughtful, dear.'

The three of them sat in silence for a while, contemplating the compass and its mysteries. In the sunlight through the tearoom window its face seemed to shimmer, and Molly could almost imagine she saw the puffs of engraved wind stir, the clouds drift idly across the stern crescent moon.

'You've got lots of sailing mementoes in the museum, Miss B,' said Arthur at last. 'Fishing nets, buoys, those old bits of scrimshaw. Maybe we could rake around and see if there are any clues?'

'Of course you can, and you're very welcome to rummage as much as you like.' Miss Badcrumble wrinkled her forehead. 'I'm sure I haven't got anything like that compass, though. I'd have remembered.'

Getting to her feet, she led Molly and Arthur back into the museum and through to a series of display cases in a gloomy corner of the second room. Rubbing dust from the glass, she pointed with a thin claw.

'This might be the best place to start. Lots of, um…nautical things.' Miss Badcrumble drew her hand back quickly. 'But I don't know a lot about them. I'm really not keen on…you know. Sailing.'

Molly smeared away more dust and examined the contents of the case. There was a brass telescope, and a sextant; a few doubloons lay arranged in an artful pile. Nothing resembled the design of the compass.

'A wooden leg!' said Arthur. 'Like Captain Ahab in *Moby-Dick*. Or like your pirate captain last night, Molly. I wonder if a sea monster ate the real leg?'

'Oh, I should hope not.' Miss Badcrumble shuddered. 'Any captain from round here would be clever enough to avoid the serpents. Perhaps it was a shark?'

Molly shot Arthur a shocked look, but decided not to press Miss Badcrumble on what she meant by that.

The old Sprye went on, 'And the leg's not wooden, dear, it's whalebone. Look, it's got carvings on it.'

So it had, Molly realised with fascination; but unfortunately they were quite crude pictures of rowing boats and skiffs, and crews with harpoons, and nothing like the engravings on the compass. She was beginning to think her find was nothing to do with the island or the mysterious ship at all, and that they were on a wild sea-goose chase.

'What are these?' Arthur was pointing at a pile of driftwood behind a frayed rope.

Miss Badcrumble twisted a wild strand of grey hair

between her talon-fingers. 'Well, now,' she murmured doubtfully. 'I'm not sure they're anything important, but I noticed they had paint on them. See? When I saw them scattered on the beach I thought sure they must have come off a boat, so I gathered them up.'

Molly started. 'Hey! That piece has eyes!'

Arthur followed her pointing finger. The shard of wood did have eyes, fierce and proud ones painted red and black. Though the paint was old and faded and peeling, they seemed to hold a glow of malevolence. Molly couldn't help feeling relieved that there was no sign of the rest of the face.

'They are a bit scary, aren't they?' observed Miss Badcrumble.

'A *bit*,' agreed Arthur dryly. 'What do you think it was, when it was in one piece?'

'Oh, I'm not at all sure,' said Miss Badcrumble, 'But I think a figurehead – off a ship, you know? Perhaps it was broken off in a storm like, well, like the one from last night.'

'That's quite possible,' said Molly. 'A boat did get

broken up on the rocks last night. I guess it's happened a lot over the years.'

'Oh dear. Did it? What a terrible thing. Well, these bits of wood are certainly interesting, but I never did find out where they came from for sure. And they don't seem to have anything to do with your compass.'

'It doesn't look like it.' Molly sighed as she pulled the heavy treasure from her rucksack again. Miss Badcrumble took it from her and turned it over, inspecting it from every angle.

'Oh!' Her taloned hand went to her mouth.

Arthur stared at her. 'What? What, Miss B?'

Molly laid her hand gently on the old woman's spindly arm and turned the compass so that she could see it. Miss Badcrumble was gaping in fright at something engraved on the back of the casing.

Molly peered. 'It's a skull and crossbones. That's what made me think it was just a souvenir. A bit of fun, you know?'

'Oh, it isn't the least bit fun.' Miss Badcrumble's

voice trembled. 'And it's not a skull, dear, not a skull at all. You see? It's an eye.'

So it was. As Molly examined it more closely, she felt a prickle at the nape of her neck. 'I've never seen anything like it. You're right – an eye and crossbones!'

'Not a particularly friendly eye, either,' remarked Arthur, looking over his shoulder. 'It reminds me of the eyes on that bit of wood. Not the same, but just as evil-looking.'

'Yes. I don't suppose there's really a connection, but it's all we've got.' Molly glanced up at Miss Badcrumble, narrowing her own eyes. 'You've seen this mark before, haven't you?'

'Oh yes. Oh yes, I have!' The old Sprye's hands were shaking. 'But it was such a long time ago. I was still a little girl. Just a child. Oh, dear.'

'Tell us,' said Arthur, pulling a bentwood chair forward for the old woman.

Molly could hear the impatience in her cousin's voice. There was expectation in the air: this could be important – it might even begin to explain where the compass had come from. Still, Molly felt sorry for Miss Badcrumble, and she hoped Arthur wouldn't scare her into silence. Fear crackled off the old Sprye like – well, like one of her magic spells. Something must have frightened her badly in the past, something connected to this symbol…

'Oh, Miss B, do sit down. Please.' Molly patted the chair. 'Tell us what happened. In your own time.'

'Yes, Molly. All right. Well, now.' Miss Badcrumble sat down gratefully, looking shaken. 'As I told you, I was just a little girl. It was a *very* long time ago; why, few people on the island now were even born! Not many humans, anyway.'

'Go on,' urged Arthur.

'I was already living with my human family.' Miss Badcrumble folded her thin fingers on her lap, beginning to relax and enjoy her story. 'In those days there were often raids, by thieves and smuggler gangs, but never one like this, oh no. The pirates couldn't be fought, they couldn't be harmed; no one could drive them away. They were supernatural creatures, you see. Ghosts!'

Ghost pirates! Molly's heart was in her throat.

'They ransacked the island from north to south, from east to west. They left nothing alone! They took gold, and jewels, and valuable things from Ravenstorm Hall. They stole food and wine, and even horses! And they stole something else, something big.'

'What?' asked Arthur and Molly together.

Miss Badcrumble lifted her eyebrows, a memory startling her. 'Why, I don't know. I only remember them carrying something wrapped up in a huge bundle, and carrying it ever so carefully. Heaven knows what it was, though.'

'Oh,' said Arthur flatly. 'And then they left and never came back, I suppose?'

'Yes. But not before I'd run into the pirate captain! I'll *never* forget *him*.' Miss Badcrumble shuddered.

'Go *on*!' Arthur was beside himself with curiosity.

'I was too young to have any sense at all. I was just like you two,' she said severely, 'wanting a bit of adventure, so I'd crept out for a closer look at the pirates. Brr! I'd seen them sail in, in their great ghostly galleon. All its sails in tatters and the eye-and-crossbones fluttering from the mast.'

Molly gasped. 'The tall ship! Miss Badcrumble, we saw it yesterday, out at sea!'

'No!' The old Sprye was aghast. 'Did it flicker in and out of sight? Vanishing, and reappearing?'

'That's the one,' confirmed Arthur. 'But tell us what happened that night, Miss B.'

'Well, there I was, out of doors on such a terrible night where I shouldn't have been. And I peeked round the corner into Kelp Street, and there *he* was! The pirate captain – right there, glaring at me! He was huge, and fierce, and he wore his hair in three braids, and his beard was all plaited and woven with dripping seaweed. But his face – oh, that was the worst! The side of it all bitten, with a row of teethmarks deep in his skin, so deep you could see bits of white bone showing through. It was horrible, but I couldn't look away, oh no. And he snarled at me – snarled like a raging wolf! – and he took his cutlass just like this,' – the old woman drew an imaginary sword from her side – 'And he grabbed me and held the blade to my throat.'

Molly and Arthur had fallen silent, riveted by the tale. Molly felt so tense she was barely able to breathe.

'"Don't you meddle in pirate business," he said to me. "Stupid child, I should chop you in pieces where you stand!"' Miss Badcrumble chopped wildly at the air with her invisible cutlass. '"But I'll let you live and warn others of Black Edward Sharksbane. For if they try to thwart me, it'll be the death of them. And of you!" And he laughed the most terrifying laugh I ever heard, and he cut a lock of my hair from beside my ear – there – and let it fall it to the ground. And then he turned, and swaggered down Kelp Street as cool as you please, and then he was gone.'

Miss Badcrumble blinked expectantly at Molly and Arthur.

'Wow,' said Art at last. 'He sounds a real charmer.'

'They say,' whispered Miss Badcrumble, 'they

say he cut the shark in bits even as it was gnawing his face.'

'Poor old shark,' said Molly.

'Bit off more than it could chew,' choked Arthur, smothering a chortle with his hand.

'It's no laughing matter,' said Miss Badcrumble, offended.

'Of course not,' said Molly, digging Arthur in the ribs.

'You mustn't cross Black Edward,' warned the old woman, her eyes wide. 'If that compass is his, he'll want it back. And you must give it to him!' She seized one of their hands in each of her spindly ones. 'You saw the ghost ship, you say? That means he's back – Black Edward Sharksbane! He'll be coming to the island, to take what's his – and what isn't.

'And when he comes, you have to promise me. Promise me you'll stay away from him! Or he might not ever let you go…'

In the dusty air and close atmosphere of the museum, it seemed for a long moment as if no one was breathing. Then, abruptly, a blackbird fluted right outside the window, breaking the spell of silence.

'Well,' declared Arthur, blowing out a sigh. 'You needn't worry, Miss B. I won't be in any hurry to introduce myself to *him*. And I suggest Molly keeps an eye on Magic Boy.'

'Yes. Jack would probably ask Black Edward for pirating tips,' said Molly. 'But listen, Miss Badcrumble, there's something we *can* try to help with. And it won't be a bit dangerous; in fact, it might stop anyone else getting hurt. We want to try to fix the old lighthouse.'

The old woman's eyes widened. 'The lighthouse? Where you found Prince Thorn trapped?'

'That's the one. Charley says it doesn't work any more. Hasn't worked for ages.'

'According to some old man down on the shore, it's cursed,' said Arthur.

'Well, yes, of course it's cursed,' said Miss Badcrumble matter-of-factly. 'The Queen of the Shadowsprye thought it was a dreadful imposition, that dazzling white light. It quite ruined the view of the stars, you know.'

'*Of course it's cursed*,' echoed Arthur, stifling another laugh as he caught Molly's eye. 'But Miss B, a little light pollution might be worth it if it stops ships getting wrecked.'

'Oh, of course, of course. But you know the Queen, dears; quite determined to have her own way. The lamp's perfectly fixable, of course, but since nobody asked me, I didn't like to interfere.

Here.' Miss Badcrumble got to her feet, shaking down her floppy skirt over her birdlike feet, and bustled through to the tearoom again. 'I know I've got it somewhere... Now, where can I have put it... Ah-hah!'

She turned from an old cabinet on the wall with a victorious smile, blowing dust and cobwebs off a small cut-glass phial, then rubbing it against her skirts. The bottle's cork was sealed with orange wax that felt sticky in Molly's fingers as Miss Badcrumble handed it to her.

'It's empty.' Molly glanced quizzically at the old Sprye.

'Not at all, no, it isn't. It's quite full up.' Retrieving it for a moment, Miss Badcrumble held the bottle up to the light and eyed it, then handed it back. 'Yes, all full up to the top. You'll see later.'

'Later?' prompted Molly.

'Later. Tonight. When it's as dark as the night will be, then you'll see. Then you'll see.'

* * *

As dark as the night will be. Molly couldn't imagine it was going to get much darker than this. Swinging her legs off the bed, she picked up her watch from the bedside table and peered at it. Just after two in the morning. Wasn't that the darkest hour, or close enough?

Once again, rain was battering the windows of Ravenstorm Hall, and she could hear the wind moaning and shrieking in the turrets. She'd gone to bed, as agreed with Arthur, in her jeans and T-shirt, so all she had to do was tug a sweater over her head and lace up her trainers, then seize her backpack. It would have been even easier if they'd still shared a room, the way they had when they first arrived – though they certainly hadn't been thrilled about it at the time. At least her cousin's room was only a little way down the corridor. When Molly tiptoed along it in the eerie darkness and pushed open the bedroom door, Arthur was waiting for her, already dressed and with a spark of excitement in his eyes.

Molly grinned. 'Hear the storm again?' she

whispered. 'We'd better take waterproofs. We'll never explain ourselves if we come home soaked to the skin.'

It was nerve-wracking to creep downstairs and through the creaky old house when Harriet was so prone to waking up, but for now the baby was silent and sleeping, and Arthur's parents must have been too exhausted to stir. The two cousins reached the front door without disturbing anyone, and from there it was a hasty run across the fields, in the driving rain, towards the cliffs and the pale lonely lighthouse.

It looked forlorn in the darkness, its unlit lamp like a blinded eye. Despite the howl and lash of the rain, Molly slowed and hesitated as she laid her hand on its little rusty gate. Then, at a nudge from Arthur, she pushed it open and they ran down the steps and shoved open the door. They almost tumbled inside in their relief at being out of the rain.

Their clothes dripped audibly in the hushed gloom. Arthur shone his torch against the curved plastered wall.

'It hasn't changed a bit,' whispered Molly.

'No,' murmured Arthur. 'You'd think no one had been in it since we were here looking for Jack. Or rather, since you and Miss B found Thorn – seeing as you two were here after I was.'

Crates and coils of rope piled against the walls, along with a stack of green glass buoys, some of them cracked. The surprisingly elegant spiral iron staircase curled up towards the deserted lamp room. Molly and Arthur's footsteps rang loudly on the stairs as they climbed up and onto the gangway that surrounded the lamp. Though the glass looked dull and dead, the faintest glow of moonlight shone sporadically between drifting clouds, letting them see one another without the torch. Arthur snapped it off.

Pulling the glass phial from his pocket, Arthur held it up. As closely as they peered into it, the bottle still seemed uselessly empty.

'It's the darkest hour,' said Molly. 'Must be. Wait till the moon goes behind a cloud, just to be on the safe side, and we'll open it.'

'I'm not sure Miss B knows what she's doing,' remarked Arthur. All the same, he picked doggedly at the old greasy wax until he'd cleared it away, then started to wiggle the cork. He frowned. 'It's really stuck. I wonder how long Miss B's had it in a cupboard.'

'Give it here.' Molly had a go, but the cork was stuck rigid; it wouldn't move even when she rather hesitantly tried to twist it with her teeth.

'I don't think we'll ever get it out,' frowned Arthur, 'and even if we did, I bet the stuff inside's evaporated. That's why it looks empty.' He turned to the lamp, and began to fiddle rather aimlessly with the mechanism. 'Oh, who knows, maybe all it needs is a good thump. That always works for my dad's laptop.'

'Don't do that— Oh!' With a cry of horror, Molly pointed out to the raging sea, blacker even than the night sky. 'Art – is that a ship?'

Arthur spun on his heel and screwed up his eyes. 'I think so – oh, I'm sure it is. Molly, it's heading straight for us. They can't see the rocks!'

That had to be true. Why else, thought Molly, would it be ploughing determinedly through the waves towards shore? Spray shot up around its bows, gleaming white, as it plunged through the swelling angry waves. The ship was nothing but a dark silhouette, but it was growing in size, coming closer every second.

Frantically Arthur tugged at the lamp, trying to force it to turn. 'Maybe it's just rusted – I can't even get it to *move*.'

'That ship's much bigger than the boat that was wrecked last night,' groaned Molly. 'There must be lots of people on board. They won't have a chance!' Once again she fought with the stopper of the phial. 'Why do they have to head this way? What are they doing?'

'Trying to get to the harbour?' Giving up, Arthur finally gave the lamp a hard kick, but it made no difference at all. The glass shuddered, but the light itself remained resolutely dull and the mechanism did not stir.

'Oh, this stupid, stupid thing!' Bursting with frustration, Molly threw the phial against the windowsill.

It shattered, sending brilliant shards of crystal flying around the lamp room. Molly and Arthur ducked as an explosion of purest silver light filled the space around them. It roiled and swirled, then shot into the dead lamp.

The light shrank into a tight, intense ball, then burst once more in a blazing dazzle, sending a brilliant white beam through the windows and across the black sea.

Molly gave a hoot of delighted triumph, and Arthur hugged her, bouncing up and down with excitement.

'Nice one, Molly! Why didn't I think of breaking it?' Arthur spun round to face the oncoming ship. 'Yes! Now it'll turn away for sure.'

Molly staggered up to lean on the window ledge beside him and peered out. 'It really worked. I don't believe it! Good old Miss Badcrumble.'

As they watched, though, their joy faded, and their

smiles turned to frowns of confusion. Taking a shocked breath, Molly blinked in disbelief.

'Why's it still coming towards us?' she asked.

Arthur shook his head slowly. 'The captain's blinded by the dazzle?'

'No,' said Molly, with a sick, plummeting feeling in her stomach. 'No, look at the ship. It's the tall ship – the ghost ship!'

Frozen to the spot, they stared at the oncoming vessel in horror. Now they could make out the rigging and the crow's-nest, and the ragged flag fluttering from the highest mast, and the proud figurehead above the shattering waves.

'It's them,' hissed Arthur. 'It's *them*.'

As the galleon sailed into the full glare of the light, the cousins could make out the crew ranged around its decks. Instead of a nervous shipful of endangered deckhands, there were hordes of armed men in shabby frock coats and breeches, swords and cutlasses brandished in their fists. The moonlight and the beam from the lighthouse looked strange as it hit them, and Molly realised this was because it wasn't shining on them at all. It was shining *through* them.

'The ghosts!' she exclaimed in horror. 'The ghost pirates, Art – they're back!'

'Just like Miss B said,' groaned Arthur. 'Oh, no – and we've guided them straight to the island.'

'I don't think they needed guiding.' Molly shivered and hugged herself, the cold and wet suddenly reaching her bones. 'They look pretty sure of where they're going.'

Arthur pointed. 'Look at the flag!'

'The eye-and-crossbones. We've got to do something!'

The ship had not even reached the harbour – it was still on the far side of the reef, where waves broke white in mid-ocean – but already the pirates were swarming overboard and down its sides. A pale army of them streamed from the decks and down from the tattered rigging, gliding across the sea as they raced smoothly towards the shore. Their running feet did not even break the water's roiling surface. As the horde reached land, rain exploded from the sky, doubling the storm's intensity, and lightning crackled overhead to turn the seascape silver.

Molly was trembling with fear, and when Arthur clutched her arm, his grip was tight with terror.

'Too late, there's nothing we can do,' Arthur said.

'No,' insisted Molly. 'We've got to try. We've got to warn the islanders.'

'OK. They might not believe ghost stories, but they'll believe their own eyes. Surely they will!'

Abandoning the lamp, which now turned smoothly as it poured light across the sea, the cousins ran clattering down the spiral stairs and out of the lighthouse. It wasn't a long run to Crowsnest, but by the time Molly and Art arrived, panting and soaked through, the spectral pirates were already on the rampage through its sleeping streets.

In their wake the storm seemed to gain new ferocious energy: rain lashed and swirled in torrents, clattering on roofs and windows, and the yowling wind tore at trees and sent signs whirling and flapping. The raucous hoots and shrieks of the raiders blended with the screaming fury of the gale.

A squat pirate sat astride a roof, ripping off slates and flinging them down into the garden below, egged on by hoots and yells from two of his mates. Another hacked with his cutlass at a young oak tree while his friend sat in its branches, shrieking with laughter. When the tree toppled, he leaped from its branches and onto the roof of a parked car, bashing a great dent in its roof. Two skinny pirates in fancy waistcoats were flinging stones and loose bricks through car windscreens; a mob of them hauled down washing lines, singing mocking songs about the ship's rigging as the ropes snapped. Two women, so alike they could be twins, danced madly on someone's rose bed, flattening the plants. A one-eyed buccaneer tossed a wheelie bin into the air and the wind caught it, as if it wanted to play along, flinging the bin and rolling and bumping it down the street out of sight.

Arthur tugged Molly's sleeve. 'The pirates! They *were* the storm last night.'

'And they're doing it again!' growled Molly.

She gasped as yellow light flooded a porch, but before she could shout a warning, a man came struggling out through the front door, wellington boots pulled on over his pyjama bottoms, desperately grasping an umbrella. He dashed down his front steps and clutched up three garden gnomes in his arms, just as a pirate picked up a fourth and flung it. It flew straight into the garden fence and shattered. One of the gnome-throwing pirates yanked at the man's umbrella and flipped it inside out, but the householder took no notice, struggling inside as the hooting raiders dragged on the umbrella's torn fabric.

'Blast this ridiculous weather!' the man cursed. With a final effort he yanked the umbrella out of the pirates' clutches, and slammed the door on them.

'I don't get it!' yelled Molly over the clamour. 'Why isn't anyone trying to fight the pirates?'

Arthur shook his head, dumbfounded, as another light snapped on in a cottage. A woman wrapped up in an oversized waterproof stumbled down her garden path and grabbed a child's bike from the lawn – just as the twin women pirates seized its wheel. She wrestled with the bike until they suddenly let go, shrieking with hilarity, and the poor woman tumbled back into a shrubbery with the bike on top of her.

'We've got to help!' shouted Arthur.

The woman staggered to her feet, clutching the child's bike and covered in mud and leaves. When she caught sight of Molly and Arthur running towards her, she waved frantically.

'What are you doing outside? Get indoors!'

'But—' began Molly.

'Heavens! It's the middle of the night. Get home before this storm gets worse! Quickly!'

As they both backed off, she stumbled inside her own front door and slammed it shut.

Molly felt Arthur grab her arm. 'I've got it!' yelled Arthur over the noise. 'They can't see the pirates – they think it's just a storm!'

Molly opened her mouth and shut it again. 'How's that possible?' she gasped at last. 'We can see them – *oh*!'

As Molly was speaking, someone crashed into her, knocking her off balance. Arthur reached to catch her, and couldn't resist a fierce sideswipe at the culprit – a woman pirate who dodged, hooting with delight, and raced on. Behind her trailed a washing line heavy with ruined and bedraggled clothes; it caught Arthur's ankles and he tumbled with Molly into a clump of prickly ornamental bushes.

Struggling to his knees, pulling aside the clinging branches, Arthur grabbed his own pebble pendant in one hand, and Molly's in the other. 'These. Don't you see?'

'Oh!' cried Molly. 'They protect us from the spell, so we can see what's really happening!'

'And feel it too,' grunted Arthur, rubbing his elbow. 'If we're the only ones who know they're here—'

'Then we're the only ones who can stop them,'

Molly shouted. She raised her hand and Arthur yanked her from the bushes. Immediately, Molly set off, pelting down the pavement and dragging Arthur by the sleeve. 'Come on!'

'They're attacking Charley's cottage!' Molly wiped streaming rain from her eyes as the two cousins skidded to a halt on Kelp Street. 'Hey! You, stop it!'

The attackers ignored her, kicking the doors and smashing branches against the windows. One of them used his cutlass to prise off the squid-shaped door knocker, giving a yelp of triumph as it came loose. He pitched it hard at one of the leaded panes. Glass exploded and the pirate gang shrieked with delight.

A howl from the roof attracted their attention, and they all shuffled back to stare up in glee. There was the same squat pirate with the hooked nose, straddling the roof and hugging the chimney pot. With a mighty wrench he tore it loose and flung it to the ground, sending the rest of the gang tumbling backwards to avoid it and laughing fit to burst. A ragged hole was left in Charley's roof, the timber roof-struts exposed to the wind and rain.

It was more than Molly could stand. She dashed into Charley's front garden, feeling a spectral chill go through her shoulder as she barged between two pirates. Swinging around, she yelled in their grinning faces.

'What are you doing? What do you *want*?'

The two pirates looked at each other; then, grinning, back at Molly. 'And who are *you* and what are *you* doing and what do *you* want?' one of them jeered. The other flapped at his face like a shocked maiden aunt.

'I'm a friend of Charley Beaumont. And this is her house you're wrecking!'

A freezing sensation swept down Molly's arm, and she yelped in fright. Turning on her heel, she saw another of the raiders gripping her shoulder and glaring down at her. He was bald-headed, with white shining eyes, and a huge hoop of gold in his left ear. She struggled, but his fingers only dug further into her skin.

'Revenge, girl,' the pirate growled. 'We're here for revenge. Don't get in our way!'

'Revenge for what? Charley's never done anything bad to you!' She'd only met the marine biologist yesterday, of course, but Molly was pretty sure that was true. 'Charley's like everyone else here. She can't even *see* you and your gang – let alone harm you!'

'Listen, mortal brat – you stay away from my men or you'll taste my cutlass!' To demonstrate, he yanked her closer and held the blade up to her mouth.

Shocked to silence, Molly saw moonlight glint on the honed edge. He might look as translucent as mist, but his grip was powerful and very real – and her shoulder was chilled to ice where he held her.

He shoved Molly away so hard, she stumbled backwards. Arthur seized her arm and helped her to her feet as the pirate loped away to make more mischief.

'What are we going to do?' Molly choked out, half-winded. She rubbed her numb shoulder. 'We can't stop them. They're going to destroy Charley's home!'

But the gang of pirates suddenly seemed to lose interest in Starfish Cottage. There was a whoop of excitement from the road beyond – a cry that sounded, Molly thought, like the howl of a destructive gale – and the pirates teemed out of the gate towards a car parked against the opposite pavement. As one they surrounded it, and began to heave, until with a mighty crash it tipped right over and rocked to a standstill, the alarm shrieking and the lights flashing. Grabbing its bumpers, singing at the tops of their raucous voices, they started to spin it on its roof.

The car's owner was staggering out of his house now, still jamming his arms into the anorak he wore over his pyjamas, but he wasn't the only one who'd been woken. Lights flicked on in the dormer window of Charley's cottage; then the sash window was hauled up and Charley herself was leaning out, her hair tousled by sleep, an expression of awed horror on her face.

'Let's get her out,' Arthur said urgently. 'She can't stay here, not with that gaping hole in her roof.'

'We can take her to Ravenstorm Hall,' Molly realised. 'Art, there has to be a reason the hall wasn't damaged last night – and I bet it's the same tonight. She'll be safe there!'

'I think I want to get back anyway.' Arthur kicked futilely at a broken slate on the grass. 'There's nothing we can do here. We haven't helped at all!'

Charley noticed them even before they had a chance to shout up to her.

'You two!' she called down, horrified. 'What are you doing out?'

'Hi, Charley!' Arthur had to cup his hands and bellow against the din. 'Come down.'

Charley withdrew from the window and it was slammed shut once more. It was only a few seconds before the front door opened and she stood there, her dressing gown dragged loosely round her shoulders and flapping in the gale. 'What is it? You should *not* be out on your own in this storm!'

Arthur just pointed up at her roof. Charley turned and gasped, and put a hand to her mouth.

'My chimney! And my window!'

'You've got to come back with us,' Molly said, grabbing her arm and eyeing the ghostly shapes of the pirates as they lost interest in the car and swarmed back towards Main Street. 'You can't stay here.'

'Seriously. There's loads of room at Ravenstorm Hall.' Arthur waved an arm in the direction of the hall. 'I know you like getting wet, but this is a bit much. Come on!'

Charley bit her lip, pale and shocked. 'All right,' she said at last, still unable to look away from the gaping tear in her roof. 'Yes. Thanks, you're right. Let me just grab a few things and I'll be right with you. And for heaven's sake, get inside the house while you wait!'

The rain was slackening, and the whoops and jeers of the pirates had faded into the distance by the time the three of them trudged wearily up the drive of Ravenstorm Hall.

'But what were you doing *out* there?' asked Charley for the umpteenth time.

'I've told you, we're into, um…meteorology. We wanted a closer look at the storm. Molly's doing a school project on, ah…climate change.'

'That's no reason to—'

'And it's just as well we came,' declared Arthur firmly. 'Or you'd be stuck in a leaking house.'

Smart move! thought Molly, with an inward grin she was too tired to show. Trust her cousin to twist things around so that Charley would feel too grateful to ask more awkward questions. And sure enough, the young woman pressed her lips together, a little crossly, and said no more about it.

Charley had insisted on lending Molly and Art extra waterproofs to wear over their drenched ones – though Molly thought it didn't really make much difference by now. She was far too damp, cold and tired to be spooked when a shadow lurched from the darkness around the hall. Besides, she was used to his sudden appearances.

'Mason. Hi.'

'Molly; Master Arthur.' His voice was ominous. 'Where have you been? I have something I need to tell you— Oh!' As he caught sight of Charley, his eyes widened.

'What?' prompted Arthur.

'Nothing! I, ah – I'm just horrified that you left the house so late. In this weather! The cliffs, you know. The lightning. Very foolish, *very* foolish, and if it happens again I'll have to wake your parents, Arthur.' His face settled into a craggy scowl. 'Don't let me catch you doing something so irresponsible again.'

'No, Mason,' said Arthur meekly.

Molly gave her cousin a surprised sidelong glance. It wasn't like Arthur to take a telling-off quite so humbly – but then Molly was sure that Mason had been about to say something else entirely. Art must have realised that the butler's reprimand was his way of hastily covering his tracks. Clearly, they would have to wait until Charley wasn't around to hear what Mason had to tell them.

'Now, inside, all of you. Miss Beaumont, I take it you've been, er…turned out of your house?' As he spoke, he hustled them all inside, his great arms spread wide around them. 'This will be the best place to shelter, yes indeed. I'll find somewhere for you to sleep.'

As soon as they were inside, he turned and slammed the door shut, locking and barring it tightly.

The sudden silence was broken only by the dripping of their clothes on the tiled floor.

'Thank you, Mason,' said Arthur. 'Don't worry about Charley, honestly. She can sleep in Molly's room, and Molly can sleep in mine. There's still a bed made up where Jack slept before.'

Mason hesitated. Then he nodded. 'Yes. Yes, very well. Excellent. Now, off to bed with you all, and no more adventures tonight, if you don't mind.' He tutted. 'So dangerous!'

They watched as he shambled off towards the kitchen, and Charley blew out a breath.

'He's a bit of a character, isn't he?' she observed. 'What on earth was *he* doing up and about, for that matter?'

'Oh, he's eccentric, that's all,' said Arthur with a dismissive wave. 'He's been here forever.'

'I bet he's got more excuse for being out late than you two,' remarked Charley, dryly. 'But I'm very grateful you were. Thanks so much – I'd have been roofless tonight if you hadn't come along.'

'Come on, then – we'll show you where Molly's room is.' Arthur yawned. 'We can sort everything out in the morning.'

'I'll second that,' said Molly, catching Art's yawn.

While Arthur sorted out Charley with her temporary room and a spare toothbrush, Molly felt the night's events catch up with her quite suddenly and headed to the spare bed, sleepiness rushing over her in a tide. She barely managed to pull off her wet clothing and climb into her blessedly dry pyjamas before crawling beneath the duvet and switching off the lamp. Art came in some time later and Molly could hear him wriggling into bed, clearly savouring the soft warm covers as much as she was.

Though her eyelids were leaden, Molly could still make out the desultory dash of the slackening rain against the window with every gust of the wind.

'I know what Mason's up to,' she muttered into the darkness at Art. 'He's out there protecting Ravenstorm Hall every night. When there's – you know – a storm…'

'Maybe,' mumbled Arthur. 'Maybe that's what gargoyles are for.'

The first hints of dawn were lightening the world outside, but they could discuss the night's events no longer. Both of them were swallowed up by sleep in seconds.

'Arthur? Molly? What's going on?' Aunt Catherine's
brisk voice dragged Molly into blurry wakefulness.

Blinking, she peeled the duvet away from her gritty
eyes, and heard Arthur give a protesting moan from
the other side of the room. Aunt Catherine stood in
the doorway, baby Harriet on her hip, looking
expectantly from one cousin to the other.

'I…uh…' Still mostly asleep, Molly could barely
remember the night's events herself.

'There's a young woman asleep in your room,
Molly. Where on earth did she come from?'

Er… Molly tried to think hard despite the sleep still
clouding her mind. *We went out to fix the lighthouse in*

the middle of the night, in a terrible storm, and rescued Charley from her dangerously damaged cottage…

Even leaving out the ghost pirates, she couldn't say that to Aunt Catherine!

Arthur managed to sit half-up, and his eyes caught Molly's across the duvet. He looked as devoid of ideas as Molly felt.

Luckily, at that very moment there was a low cough from behind Aunt Catherine, and she turned on her heel. 'Oh. Good morning, Mason. Have *you* any idea what's going on?'

His face was very serious and solemn. 'I do hope you don't mind, Mrs Wolfrey. Young Miss Beaumont's house was badly damaged in the storm last night, so I invited her to stay at the hall. Just an emergency measure, and I was sure you'd understand. If you like, I can find someone else to take her in tonight…'

'Oh, no,' said Aunt Catherine hurriedly. 'No, of course that's fine, Mason. How dreadful for her. Miss Beaumont's very welcome here, and she can stay as long as she needs to.'

Exhausted, Molly couldn't help slumping back into the cosy bed, but she caught Mason's eye and gave him a grateful smile. Arthur managed to sit up straight on the edge of the bed, and he stretched, yawning.

'Morning, Mum. Morning, Harriet.' He stumbled up to give his mother a brief sleepy hug, and tickle Harriet's toes. The baby mewled in cross protest and gave Arthur an odd, piercing stare.

'Oh dear. You look like the storm kept you up all night. And Molly, it's so nice of you to give up your room for Charley.' Aunt Catherine looked sympathetic, and Molly felt a little stab of guilt.

If only you knew...

'Why don't you stay in bed a little longer, and I'll get some bacon on?' Aunt Catherine went on kindly. 'You too, Arthur. Go on back under the covers, and join us when you're in the land of the living.'

Now they were awake, though, both Molly and Arthur were too hungry to go back to sleep, and they managed to stagger blearily into their clothes and make their way down to the kitchen. The smell of frying bacon was irresistible, and when they opened the door Charley was already at the table, her smile surprisingly cheerful.

'Morning! Thanks so much for letting Mason give me your room, Molly.' Charley gave them a wink behind Aunt Catherine's back.

Oh good, thought Molly, *at least we've all got our stories straight!* The black metal hands on the huge old railway clock on the wall showed half-past ten. *Well, that's nearly six hours' sleep, anyway...*

Uncle Bill sat at the head of the table surrounded by small bottles of cleaning fluid and many scattered cotton-buds. In front of him was an ornate baroque urn that he was cleaning delicately, peering over his half-moon glasses. 'Afternoon, lazybones. Jack and I have been up for hours, haven't we, young man?'

Jack grinned and carried on scrawling with his crayons on a drawing pad.

'Oh, now leave them alone. They had a rough

night.' Aunt Catherine set bacon sandwiches down in front of Molly and Art and then Charley. 'There, that'll put you right, sleepyheads.'

'I hope you've got one for yourself, Catherine,' said Charley. 'I bet little Harriet keeps you awake, too.'

Aunt Catherine gave a rueful smile. 'She's a bit unsettled just now, that's for sure. I hope she grows out of it soon.' She frowned with concern at her grizzling daughter, still clinging to her hip. 'Hopefully it's just a phase, like Nurse Martha said.'

'We didn't tell you about the nurse's verdict, did we, Arthur?' Uncle Bill put down his cotton bud and scratched his head. 'She says that Harriet's growing a little faster than is normal for a baby her age.'

'Is that what's making her so grumpy?' Molly asked, squeezing ketchup onto her bacon sandwich.

'Nurse Martha seems to think so. Poor Harriet,' Aunt Catherine said, gently jiggling Harriet up and down, which only earned her another fierce baby glare. 'I don't blame you for being a bit out of sorts.'

'We'll do the washing-up,' said Charley firmly.

'Won't we, guys? It's so kind of you to let me stay, Catherine.'

'Well, I'd appreciate that,' admitted Aunt Catherine. 'Bill and I need to get some work done this morning. But I expect you'll want to go down to the village soon and check on your cottage.'

'I'd better.' Charley gave a rueful sigh. 'I'm kind of dreading what I'll find, though. It was pitch dark when I left.'

Uncle Bill gave her a sympathetic glance. 'I'll come down later and give you a hand clearing up.'

'Oh, bless you. You're both lifesavers.'

'I just hope there isn't a third storm tonight.' Uncle Bill shook his head. 'It's getting ridiculous. How Ravenstorm Hall's escaped any damage is beyond me. Maybe Molly's casting magic spells!'

'And me!' interjected Jack.

'And you, Small Incredible Cornell.'

Molly didn't dare catch Arthur's eye. There might be magic around, but it was nothing to do with her or Jack...

'I hope no more shipping was damaged last night,' said Charley, sipping her coffee.

'No, it wasn't. I checked earlier when I called the post office. More property damage, but no wrecks.' Uncle Bill shook his head and dipped a cotton-bud into a vial. 'That's something to be grateful for, anyway.'

This time Molly shot a look at Arthur. *Maybe our visit to the lighthouse wasn't completely wasted, after all.*

Arthur grinned back, understanding, then turned to Jack. 'What's that you're drawing, Magic Boy?' He leaned across to look. 'Yuck! Is that a monster?'

Jack was indignant. 'It's a giant squid. A *real* squid. It's for Charley.'

'Oh!' Charley took the drawing, delighted. 'Jack, how did you know? Squid are my favourite sea creature.'

'I guessed,' he told her proudly. 'You've got a squid on your door.'

'So I have! You're very observant, young man. You'd make a great marine biologist.'

Jack swelled visibly, but Molly's stomach wrenched. Charley would find out soon enough that she didn't have a squid knocker any more. Not fixed to her door, anyway.

Charley pointed to the scribbled background. 'Look at this, Jack. You've done a fantastic job here. You've drawn it deep underwater, and that's exactly where squid live. That's what makes them so mysterious and hard to find.'

'Yes, dark blue, see? I thought that'd look deep. And that's the sand, and that's a bit of a shipwreck. Sort of.'

'You're brilliant.' Charley gave him a hug. 'I'm going to stick it on my fridge.'

When the washing-up was done, and the plates and pans stowed away, Charley gave a sigh and wiped her hands on the dishtowel. Aunt Catherine and Uncle Bill had vanished to their office, having settled the grouchy Harriet to an uneasy nap, and with several reminders to Charley that she must stay at the hall as long as she needed to.

'But in the meantime,' Charley told them with a sigh, 'I suppose I ought to go back to Starfish Cottage.' Glumly she added, 'I'd better steel myself for what I'll find.'

'We'll walk you down the drive,' offered Arthur. 'I'm still a bit woozy – how about you, Molly? The fresh air will do us some good.'

Outside, there was still no sign, apart from a few stripped leaves, that the storm had hit the island so violently just hours ago. Small clouds scudded in a clean blue sky, and the breeze was warm and light. Ravenstorm Hall and its towering turrets were untouched, every slate in place.

'Thanks for not telling on us,' Arthur said to Charley. 'We'd have been in serious trouble.'

'Oh, don't worry. I'm good at keeping secrets.' Charley winked. 'Though I still don't know what you thought you were doing.'

'Safer if you don't know,' Arthur told her, pulling an ominous face.

Charley laughed. 'All right, all right. I'm glad you

came along. Just be careful, OK?'

'We promise,' said Molly, crossing her fingers behind her back. There really wasn't much chance of being careful around ghost pirates, after all.

'And since it all sounds a bit serious, let me know if I can help. I'll be back later – I think I'm going to take up your mum's offer to stay a few nights, Art.'

'That's great.' Arthur grinned. 'See you later.'

They waved at Charley as she set off down the road, then turned back up the Ravenstorm Hall drive. Instantly, Arthur pointed up at one of the high turrets and exclaimed in surprise.

'There's Mason!'

'So it is.' Molly shaded her eyes against the sunlight. The butler was framed in one of the pointed gothic windows, and as they watched he swung it open and beckoned to them.

Arthur nudged Molly. 'I knew it. He's got something to tell us!'

'Whatever he didn't want to say in front of

Charley, last night,' agreed Molly. 'Ha! I knew he wasn't really cross with us.'

There was a heavy side door that led into that particular corner of Ravenstorm Hall, as they'd discovered on their rainy-day explorations. Molly headed straight for it, Art close behind. Molly twisted the black iron handle and shoved it open with some difficulty. It creaked ominously. The passageway and stairs ahead of them were dark with shadows, and chilly after the warmth of the sun outside. The whole place smelt of dust and old paper.

'It's like no one had been in this part of the house for years,' said Molly.

'But it's where Mason's rooms are,' pointed out Arthur, 'so that can't be true.'

Molly led the way up the winding stairwell, ducking cobwebs and listening to the echo of their scuffing footsteps. They were both a little out of breath when the stone stairs finally ended in an iron-bound oak door. It creaked open, and there stood Mason, smiling in his usual gloomy way.

'There you are. Come in.' He gestured with his huge hand, and they slipped past him as the door clunked shut behind them.

Molly gazed around in fascination. The air here was as dry and dusty as it was on the stairs, and just as cool. She rubbed her bare arms. The centrepiece in the room was a massive oak desk, covered in layers of grime and blots of ink, with piles of scrolls and paper and what looked like real old-fashioned parchment, crumbling at the edges. Around the walls were stacked more scrolls and ancient books, as well as pieces she suspected Aunt Catherine and Uncle Bill would love – a grandfather clock, tall mahogany bookcases, a roll-top desk. Against one corner stood a mirror, stained and fly-blown and framed in ornate silver; reflected in it was a vast marble fireplace carved with lions and angels, the mantelpiece held aloft by cherubs whose chubby cheeks were grubby with ancient coal dust. Everywhere there were statues and ornaments of mythical creatures, some she recognised and some she didn't want to. There was even a giant-sized human skull with a candle stuck on top.

'This is – cosy,' said Molly politely.

'It's home.' Mason smiled, obviously rather pleased. 'Won't you sit down?'

Having offered, he then searched around rather vaguely for some chairs. He found a battered leather armchair, into which Arthur almost disappeared, and flung papers and books off a red-velvet upholstered sofa for Molly. Mason himself simply leaned against the massive desk, his features grim once more.

'You've seen the pirates,' he said without preamble. 'So, Master Arthur, Molly: you know the danger that threatens Ravenstorm Island.'

Molly leaned forward eagerly on the sofa. 'We saw them last night, trashing the village.'

'Indeed.' His lips curled in a slight smile. '"Trashing" Crowsnest, as you say, and not for the first time.'

'But not Ravenstorm Hall,' put in Arthur. 'They

didn't harm this place.'

'Quite. I hardly think they'd dare.' His gloomy mouth twitched again.

'You protect it, don't you, Mason?' asked Molly. 'That's why we saw you patrolling the grounds.'

He nodded heavily. 'It's true; I can protect the hall from their raids, at least. It's all I can do now, and I cannot help the village or the rest of the island. There was a time when all the gargoyles of Ravenstorm Hall had to come together to protect their island home. A great evil threatened it, you see – a much greater evil than the pirate raiders.'

'I don't think I want to know,' murmured Molly.

'Indeed, and we must hope it never comes again,' Mason said gravely. 'We drove it off once, and that was enough.'

'But I don't understand.' Arthur pointed at the window. 'If you drove away something much worse than the pirates before, why can't you get rid of them now? There must be enough gargoyles on Ravenstorm Hall to defend the entire island.'

Mason sighed and shook his head. 'It isn't like that, Master Arthur, not any more. The gargoyles have all been turned to stone, you see. Permanently petrified. I'm the only one who is free, and sometimes even I have to return to my place with the others to rest. The gargoyles can't help Ravenstorm Island, not now.'

Molly stood up and went to the window. Looking out, she could see a row of the fierce stone gargoyles crouched above the west wing. Suddenly they seemed not ferocious or frightening, but terribly sad.

'But what happened? How did they get turned to stone? Was it the Queen of the Shadowsprye again? If I'd known, I would have saved some of her magic potion – the one that brought the stone children back to life.'

'I'm afraid not.' Mason gave a deep sigh. 'It wasn't the Queen who laid her curse on the gargoyles, so there's no point looking to her for help – even if she'd do it. And she's never been fond of gargoyles.'

'But who, then?' asked Arthur.

'Ah.' Mason's grey eyes grew distant, shadowed and sad. '*She* cursed the gargoyles for what they did. And who could blame her? The stone curse was not so strongly laid on me, and I could live and move – but she cursed me never to leave the grounds of Ravenstorm Hall again. Here I must stay, and stay forever.'

'But who is she?' demanded Arthur.

Both cousins watched the butler intently as his lips parted. A breath sighed out, and his facial muscles tightened with effort. Mason frowned, and tried once more, licking his lips. But when he managed at last to speak, his words seemed to catch horribly in his throat.

'*Cahh-kkaaaaahhh…*'

Arthur gasped in horror, and Molly's hands went to her mouth. It wasn't a human sound at all; it was like a cry from the ravens up in the turrets. Alarmed, Molly reached out a hand towards him, but all Mason did was shake his head with a wry smile.

'Ah, I can't say her name. That's part of the magic;

and nor can I tell you more. But we all deserved what she did, oh yes. And why should she have forgiven me? I shall never forgive myself.'

The two cousins stared at him in silence. Molly felt a huge wave of sadness for Mason, trapped forever in Ravenstorm Hall, his friends turned to stone around him.

'I can't tell you more.' He shook his heavy head. 'I'm sorry. But perhaps you can find a way to protect the village, and the rest of Ravenstorm Island. Perhaps you can even help the gargoyles somehow.'

'Do you think so?' asked Molly eagerly.

Mason only nodded.

Arthur narrowed his eyes. 'Mason. Are you trying to tell us something?'

Once again, that brief nod of the head, and Mason's eyes met Molly's steadily.

'But can't you tell us *more*?' exclaimed Arthur in frustration.

The butler shrugged, and frowned, and opened his mouth.

'*Cahh-kkaaaaahhh…*'

'Oh, Mason.' Stepping forward, Molly took his hand and squeezed it sympathetically. Was it tears she saw shining in the grim old gargoyle's eyes? 'He can't tell us, Arthur. He literally can't.'

'We'll do our best, Mason.' Arthur touched his arm gently. 'We really will. You can count on us.'

Feeling more sorry than Molly would have believed possible for the huge stony-faced butler, the two of them said their goodbyes and made their way back down the winding stairwell.

Once they were well out of his earshot, Arthur said, 'I think we should go and ask Miss Badcrumble.' He pushed aside another cobweb. 'She obviously knows Mason – or at least, about him – so perhaps she can help.'

'There has to be some connection.' Molly frowned. 'Between getting rid of the pirates, and freeing the gargoyles. The woman who cursed them must be something to do with the pirates. Otherwise why would he have said what he did? That we might be able to help the gargoyles, too?'

'I just wish he could tell us *something*,' grumbled Arthur, 'but it isn't his fault. Anyway, Miss B managed to lift the curse on the lighthouse, no problem. Maybe she can do the same for the curse on Mason's friends?'

'I've a feeling it won't be that simple,' said Molly glumly, 'but we might as well try.'

'Miss B! Miss Badcrumble!' Arthur thumped his fist on the museum's door again.

Molly stepped back and squinted up at the roof and windows of the rambling little house. A seagull stood on the chimney-pot, stretching its wings and whinging mournfully. 'She can't be in. She always answers eventually.'

'Unless she's fallen off that stepladder she insists on climbing.'

'Oh, I hope not!'

'No, I'm sure she hasn't. Just kidding.' Arthur gave up knocking, and rubbed his bruised fingers. 'I suppose she could be off at that sea-cave again, feeling homesick for Shadowsprye land. Or at the well where she hid the children's photos before.'

Molly was doubtful. 'I suppose. But this is an emergency. We've got to find out something before tonight. I don't care what the weather forecast says, I'll bet you anything there's another storm coming.'

Arthur suddenly glanced over his shoulder at the road beyond. 'I don't think she'd mind if we just looked around, do you?'

'I'm sure she wouldn't. *If* we could actually get in,' Molly pointed out.

'We can.' Arthur grinned and pointed at the tea room window. It was cracked open to the fresh air and the breeze.

'Art! You wouldn't.'

As it turned out, Art most certainly would. After scanning the road carefully for passers-by, he hitched himself up on Molly's cupped hands, pulled the window wider, and slithered through. Molly heard a faint, 'Ouch!' and a thump as he hit the floor, and then Arthur's footsteps faded. In seconds he reappeared at the door, swinging it wide and inviting Molly in with a sweep of his arm.

'I'm not sure we should be doing this.' But Molly picked up the backpack she'd set down, squeezed inside quickly and closed the door.

'You know, I'm not joking – I don't think Miss B would mind,' Art was saying. 'It *is* an emergency, like you said. And another thing – I've got a bad feeling about her being away. I don't think she's just off somewhere pining for the other Shadowsprye.'

Molly didn't like to agree with Arthur's reasoning, but she had to admit she'd been getting the same feeling. Crossing to the counter where the old Sprye served her teas, she lifted a delicate china mug with a flowery pattern and a curlicued handle.

'Look. This milk's only half-drunk. And she didn't clear it away.'

Arthur came to her side, wrinkling his nose as he dipped a fingertip into the congealed liquid. 'There's a skin on it. Have you ever heard of Miss B *not* finishing a cup of warm milk?' He shook the slimy film off his fingers in distaste. 'Something's up, Moll. We'd better investigate.'

'Well, we'll just have a quick look around,' Molly muttered. 'And we'd better not touch anything precious.'

'Course not.'

They called and shouted as loudly as they dared through the tearoom and the small flat beyond, which was where Miss Badcrumble lived. But as they'd feared, the old woman was nowhere to be found. At last they returned, dejected, to the tea room.

'There's nothing,' said Molly. 'Maybe she's visiting relatives…'

Arthur's eyes widened and he gave an exclamation of shock. 'No. Look at these!' He hurried over to a table and lifted something, looking half-triumphant, half-scared. 'Look. Miss B's gloves!' He waved them in Molly's face. 'Never mind the milk, this is *proof*. Something's definitely wrong, Moll. Miss B never goes anywhere without her gloves!'

Molly nodded slowly, a horrible feeling creeping up her spine. 'You're right. Something's happened! Let's take a look in the museum, see if there's any clues.'

The Museum of Curiosities was sunk into even deeper gloom than usual. Even when Arthur snapped on all the available lamps, darkness still hung threateningly in the corners, and dust motes danced in the weak pools of light. But it was clear at once that something was terribly wrong. Shelves had been toppled over, leaning drunkenly against one another, spilling books and old albums across the floor. Fragments of shells and old crystal and pottery lay scattered at their feet; crates and boxes and cabinets had been tossed around, their contents jumbled, their glass covers smashed.

'What a mess,' breathed Molly. 'What happened here?'

'It's not Miss B's usual chaos, that's for sure.' Arthur shook his head grimly. 'Pirates, at a guess. *That's* what's happened.'

Shocked into silence, the two cousins crept forward, shoving boxes out of the way, lifting shelves, nudging broken glass carefully aside with their trainers. Molly felt her heart thudding.

'What if they're still here?' whispered Arthur, sounding uncharacteristically nervous.

'I don't think so,' whispered Molly back. 'The weather's fine outside, and they'd be making a lot more noise.'

'All the same – let's be careful…'

Molly pushed aside an old fish-crate and wriggled between fallen shelves into the next aisle. As her eyes adjusted to the gathered pools of darkness, she took a breath.

'Art, come here!' called Molly, suddenly not caring how much noise they made. 'All the nautical exhibits – they're gone!'

Arthur levered a broken shelf out of his way and clambered over the crates to Molly's side. He stared at the ravaged display cases. The brass telescope was gone, and the sextant; even the scraps of painted driftwood had vanished.

'It's all been taken,' said Molly, her scalp prickling with fear. 'And so has...' She swallowed hard, unable to say the old Sprye's name.

Arthur crouched to pick up a scrap of an old photograph, anger clouding his eyes. 'This isn't like their other mischief, is it? It's not just mindless *vandalism*. They messed the place up but they didn't take anything from the other shelves. Don't you get the feeling they were looking for something?'

Slowly Molly slipped her pack off her shoulder, and unclipped the straps. She reached in and drew out the beach towel, then unwrapped it. The compass lay, gleaming dully, in her shaking hands.

'What if they were looking for this?' she whispered. 'And they couldn't find it?'

'The compass has to be something to do with all this.' Arthur shook his head grimly. 'The way Mason reacted to it, and everything. I'll bet the compass is exactly what they were looking for.'

'And when they couldn't find it, they took Miss

Badcrumble. Oh, Arthur. This is our fault! We can't leave her to the pirates.'

Arthur ground his teeth. 'And we can't hide up at the hall every night while the pirates loot the whole island. It could go on for weeks – for ever!'

'Then we have to stop them.' Molly felt a sudden steely resolve. 'We can't wait for them to do it all over again, and we can't let them take Miss Badcrumble away. What if they keep her captive forever, just out of spite? What if they—' Molly bit her lip. She couldn't bear to say the words out loud.

'They won't kill her, if that's what you're thinking. They still think she has something they want.'

'Well, there's only one thing to do. We have to go and save her!' Molly's confidence wavered, and her face fell. 'But how will we get to them?'

Arthur winked. 'I know how,' he told Molly. 'But first we're going to have to borrow something from Charley…'

'Oh no.' Charley shook her head violently. 'Are you two crazy? I'm not letting the three of you have my boat!'

Molly Art and Jack stood facing the marine biologist in the wreckage of her cottage, the furniture soaked and the roof gaping to the sky, the squid door knocker clutched in her hands. Charley looked fierce and severe and completely determined. But there was nothing more stubborn and determined than Arthur, thought Molly, when he really wanted something.

'You promised you'd keep our secrets, Charley.'

'Well, yes. *Yes*. But this isn't what I meant! I didn't promise I'd help you out with any crazy schemes.

And I *certainly* never said you could have my boat!'

'The sea's perfectly calm. It's only for an hour! I thought – we thought you'd approve. It's Molly's climate change project! And Jack would love a boat trip so much…'

Gosh, thought Molly, amused despite her anxiousness about her cousin's plan. *Arthur can do amazing puppy-eyes.* Molly stifled a giggle as she saw her brother gazing up sweetly as Charley in perfect imitation of his cousin. *And so can Jack.* Her little brother was clearly just as eager to get out on that boat as Art was.

Her cousin pressed his advantage. 'Don't you want to help, Charley? See, we've got this theory about the storms! And what's causing them!'

'Lovely. You have very enquiring minds and that's *wonderful*, but you are *not* getting your hands on my boat.'

'You said that kids our age go out on the sea around Ravenstorm Island all the time,' Molly pointed out.

'Well…yes, that's true, but that's when the

weather's behaving itself. And it only applies to children who live here and have had proper training. You can't even drive a motorboat!'

'Actually, I do live here now, and I can drive it,' said Art smugly. 'I did this adventure training thing last term at school. I learned all about motorboats and I'm perfectly capable of driving one. I've got my certificate and everything.'

'Your parents are paying too much for that school,' Charley growled. 'I don't care how calm the sea is, and I don't care if you're Popeye the Sailor Man, you're not getting in my boat!'

Which just went to show, thought Molly, how much Charley knew about trying to say no to Arthur. Another half-hour's pleading and cajoling and moral blackmail, and Charley surrendered the spare keys with an exclamation of exasperated defeat.

'No going beyond the bay! Is that clear? Not so much as a boat-length, Arthur!'

'Course not, Charley. You won't regret this, I promise.'

'I bet I will. Just don't make me have to break any bad news to your parents!'

True to Arthur's word, though, the three of them spent a happy afternoon motoring peacefully and obediently in the bay. There was no sign of pirates or any ghost ship, of course, but Jack was more than content spotting dolphins and seals, and fishing with his crab line.

Arthur turned out to be very capable, and very responsible too. Even Charley had to admit that when they got back to the jetty.

'Well, well,' said Charley, shutting one eye. 'Not a scratch. You've been as good as your word, Arthur. I admit I had my doubts.'

'Oh, I know.' Arthur grinned. 'And I don't blame you, really. I mean, most people our age can't work a motorboat. But I told you I was good at this.'

'Not a scratch on her,' muttered Charley again as she walked the length of her boat, eyeing the hull. 'And nobody even fell in.'

'Course not,' said Arthur complacently. 'Now we

really ought to get back to Ravenstorm Hall. I don't want my parents to worry.'

Charley raised an eyebrow with a half-smile. 'Who'd have thought you'd be the responsible type, Art?'

And amidst all that grudging praise, thought Molly as they hurried away with swift farewells, it was no wonder Charley had forgotten to ask for her keys back.

Arthur was looking a lot less responsible now. Maybe it was a trick of the intermittent moonlight, but Molly could see a devil-may-care gleam in her cousin's eyes as he steered the little motor launch out across the black night-time sea, and Arthur hooted with delight whenever a wave broke over the bows. Molly crouched below the gunwale in her waterproofs against the rising wind and rain. She hugged her backpack tightly; it wouldn't do to lose the contents now. What if the compass ended up at the bottom of the ocean where no one could find it – what might the pirates do then?

'They must be coming again,' yelled Arthur. 'Look at this weather!' He pointed ahead with one hand, gripping on tight to the rudder with the other. 'Hang on, the waves are getting huge out here…'

Molly winced as she looked over the side and saw an alarmingly enormous wave surging up in front of them. She seized the side of the boat and braced herself…but the wave seemed to part in front of them, letting Charley's boat through without so much as a jolt.

'What was that?' she called back to Arthur.

'I dunno.' Arthur tried to sweep the soaking hair out of his eyes and squinted into the wind. 'It's like the storm looks much worse than it actually is.'

'Oh,' Molly gasped, and she pulled out her Ravenstorm Island token from the neck of her T-shirt. 'It's the tokens again! We must be getting close, this storm is magical and it's not affecting us.'

'Well, don't let go of it,' Arthur grinned as another sheet of rain lashed his face. 'I'd hate to see what this would be like if the storm *was* affecting us. Any sign of the ship?'

Molly scrambled up onto her hands and knees, narrowing her eyes against the wind. 'Yes! I can see its outline – there, straight ahead!'

Arthur had taken a wide circle once he'd passed the reef and its breaking waves, and they were approaching the pirate ship from the stern. His hair whipped back from his face, holding vertical like an image of some crazed scientist.

Molly felt a shudder of fear as she saw the crew lined up once again, shaking their cutlasses and yelling in anticipation of another raid, but they were all looking towards the island, eager for booty. Their eye-and-crossbones banner fluttered arrogantly in the gale. None of the pirates glanced at the little launch that bobbed against their sides as Arthur cut the motor.

Arthur's eyes were narrowed in concentration as he focused on keeping the motorboat close beneath the great galleon. There was a yell of command from amidships, a terrifyingly harsh and cruel voice that drowned even the storm.

'They've lit our way, mates! They're welcoming us in Crowsnest tonight!'

A roar of laughter went up. Sure enough, the revived lighthouse lamp swept a steady beam of silver across the sea, illuminating the pirates in all their grisly glory. The crew swarmed down the rigging once again and leaped over the gunwales, sweeping as lightly and lethally as mist across the churning waves, and towards the harbour and the village.

Molly peered up towards the ship. The man gripping the rail and watching his men was a fearsome sight, his russet hair braided into three long ropes, his beard tangled with dripping seaweed. When he drew his own cutlass, the beam from the lighthouse gleamed from it, and Molly saw his face very clearly; savage and brutal, with the curving punctures of a bite mark running down the side of his head. Patches of white bone showed through where the teeth had gone deepest.

Black Edward Sharksbane! she thought, too awed to be truly frightened. As she watched, the ferocious captain gave another yell and leaped down from the forecastle to the main deck; then he was overboard and racing across the sea, overtaking his men and leading them on towards the island.

Molly was sure he was responsible for Miss Badcrumble's disappearance; more than likely the old Sprye was held captive on board this terrible ship. What was it Miss Badcrumble had said, about the first raid all those years ago? The young Sprye changeling had confronted the dreadful captain in the streets of Crowsnest, and his men had been carrying something. *Something wrapped up in a huge bundle, and carrying it ever so carefully.* Perhaps that was here too, whatever it was.

Molly retreated from the boat's side and stowed her pack firmly in the cabin, hoping it wouldn't be found – even if they were. She made her way back to Arthur at the wheel. 'I think they've all gone,' she whispered. 'It must be safe to go on board, if we can.'

'As safe as it will ever be,' muttered Arthur. 'No, wait! Look.'

From beside the wheel, Molly could see what her cousin saw: three familiar figures lolling on the quarterdeck. One of them stood up and stretched. He was bald, with white shining eyes, and a huge hoop of gold gleamed in his left ear.

Molly would have recognised him anywhere: the terrifying man with the cutlass who had threatened her at Starfish Cottage. And his two friends were the skinny pirates she had shoved past, trying to stop them. She shuddered as she remembered the icy touch of their ghostly bodies.

As she watched, one of pirates got up to do a little jig, then settled to picking his nose. His friend sneered at something, and the nose-picker whacked angrily at him with a scrawny hand. Gold-Hoop barked at the pair, and they settled down, scowling.

'Sharksbane must have left them on guard, now that they've got a prisoner,' whispered Arthur. 'We'll have to be very careful. Come on.'

'Do you think we'll be able to board the ship?' wondered Molly. 'Will it be touchable, like the pirates? Or will we fall straight through it and into the water?'

'There's only one way to find out.' Arthur had a coil of rope over his shoulder, and as Charley's boat drifted back into the shadows at the stern, he uncoiled the end and fashioned a loop in it. Then, taking a deep breath, he threw it up towards the rail.

Molly could see what he was aiming for: a jutting spar of wood that was probably added for the very purpose of holding a mooring rope. Arthur's throw missed, thudding back onto the motorboat's deck, and Molly felt her heart flip. Once more Arthur tried and failed; then on the third try the rope sailed gracefully up, straight towards its target, and Arthur's makeshift lasso caught tightly around the spar.

Grinning, Arthur coiled the other end into a knot and tugged it tight around a cleat. 'I don't care what Charley says, I love my school. Let's go.'

He grabbed the rope in both hands and shinned up

it, his feet scrabbling against the shimmering hull of the ship. The rope held firm, and his trainers scuffed the painted wood. Molly waited until her cousin had reached the top and then climbed up after him, hauling herself over the rail. The two cousins collapsed onto the deck and Molly caught her breath, waiting in case there was some sign that those vicious guards had heard them.

But there was another sound on the air around the decks, and it must have drowned out the noise of their arrival. It was a mournful note, swelling and dying, sad and eerie in the cold darkness.

'What's that?' whispered Arthur.

A cold ripple of unease went down Molly's spine, and she shook herself. 'I don't know, but I'm not sure I like it. Let's look for Miss Badcrumble. The sooner we're off this ship, the better.'

She didn't hold out much hope of finding the old woman quickly, though. An age seemed to pass as Molly and Art crept on silent feet across the decks, pausing with their hearts in their mouths when a board creaked, and ducking back into the shadows when the guards happened to turn their way. They peered behind barrels that stank of fish, pulled aside great heaps and coils of barnacled rope, even clambered a few metres up the rigging to look around; but there was no sign of their friend. Molly was beginning to think their cause was hopeless when Arthur nudged her and hissed.

'That sound again. Listen!'

Molly cocked her ear. Yes: it was that unhappy song once more, the notes lilting out into the darkness as a woman sang of her home, and how much she missed it.

'Ah, shaddup!' barked one of the guards, and kicked a barrel.

But the singer took no notice. The song rose again, sad and sweet as a violin, making Molly's heart clench with sorrow.

'Do you think…' began Arthur, then frowned. 'That can't be Miss B, surely. I'm pretty sure she doesn't sing. Not like that, anyway.'

'I don't think so,' whispered Molly. 'But what if it's the thing she saw the pirates take? A big bundle, remember? What if they kidnapped one of the islanders, and she's still here? Held prisoner *all these years*?'

They gazed at one another in horror.

'We've got to look,' said Arthur. 'We've got to at least find out.'

'We can't abandon whoever's singing, anyway,' whispered Molly. 'She sounds so sad and desperate.'

Arthur raised his head above the great chests they were hiding behind. The guards were distracted, shouting angry words at the singer, and Arthur gave Molly a nod. They crept out on silent feet, ducking beneath the furled sails as they passed close to the guards.

'That way,' whispered Molly, pointing toward the prow.

A flight of wooden steps led past what looked like the captain's cabin door, with its elegant paned glass and glowing hurricane lamps within. For long seconds Molly and Art were blinded as the silver beam of the lighthouse swept across them, but then Molly scrambled up into the shadows on the forecastle. It was even darker after that shaft of brilliance. Miss Badcrumble had been just a little too efficient with her potion, thought Molly dryly.

They crouched against the foremast, keeping very still. 'It's louder than ever here,' said Molly softly, as the song pricked tears in her eyes. 'She must be close.'

'I don't see anyone.' On hands and knees, Arthur crawled forward until he was nearly at the bowsprit. Molly scuttled forward to her cousin's side. Surely the singer had to be nearby; it sounded as if the mournful music was coming from right beside her…

Molly looked up at the carved forepeak at the prow of the ship, and gasped. 'It's the figurehead!'

'Well, yes, we're at the front—'

'No, Art – it's the figurehead that's *singing*.'

They leaned over the rail, one on each side of the prow, and stared up astonished at the beautiful carved woman. It was obvious she hadn't been carved as part of the ship – there were chains looped tightly around her, fixed with heavy padlocks, fastening her in position. Her hair was long and red and flowing, and gleamed like copper ore in rock. There was a silvery-grey sheen to her skin, and to the small wings that sprouted from her shoulder blades. Molly clasped her hand over her mouth.

'She isn't wooden, Art.' Gently Molly reached up to touch the tip of a bat-like wing. 'She's made of stone.'

The music stopped abruptly as the figurehead's eyes snapped open. They were as blue and hard and shining as lapis lazuli. Molly bit her lip, holding her breath as the woman turned her head. The sound of stone scraping against iron chain was somehow even sadder than her song.

'You're a gargoyle!' exclaimed Arthur in shock.

Now the woman's eyes were wide and afraid. 'Who are you?'

'Friends!' Molly reassured her. 'We're friends. We know other gargoyles!'

The woman looked from her to Arthur and back again, teeth biting on her lip. Then, very suddenly, her lips curved in a smile and something like a tear shone at the corner of her eye.

'Friends!' she whispered. 'It's been such a long time since I saw one of those.'

Feeling terribly sorry for her, Molly touched the great heavy links of the chain. Rust from it had scraped against her stony skin and left reddish streaks. 'You're a prisoner,' she murmured.

'Yes. I've been one for a long time. But maybe – maybe not now?' There was a terrible mixture of hope and doubt in her voice. 'Would you—'

'Would we?' exclaimed Arthur under his breath. 'Anyone who these hooligan pirates don't like is a friend of ours. Eh, Molly?' He seized the rusty chain in his fist and tugged.

'You bet!' said Molly fiercely. She pulled Arthur's hand away. 'Not like that, you'll make it tighter. Look for the locks.'

A raucous voice drifted up from the quarterdeck.

'Finally shut up, have you? I hope you've lost yer voice!'

There was a roar of laughter from the pirate guards, and the three of them held their breath. Then the figurehead murmured, 'Now's the time, then. Can you do it?'

Molly nodded, running her hands up the chains until she found the padlocks that secured them. 'My dad's an escapologist – some of the time,' she whispered proudly. 'He showed me how to do this…!'

Molly pulled a hairgrip from her pocket and started to pinch the rubber tips off with her fingernails. Arthur watched with fascination, but his questions were all for the gargoyle woman.

'How did you end up here? What on earth happened to you?'

'Oh,' the woman sighed softly, 'that's such a long and long-ago story…'

'Well, tell it to us while Molly gets you free. Otherwise I don't think I can stand the suspense,'

Arthur said. 'What's your name, by the way? I'm Arthur – and Houdini here is the Incredible Molly Cornell.'

'And I'm Nancy.' The woman gave a soft shaky laugh as she squirmed to let Molly get at a padlock. 'I came from Ravenstorm Island.'

'Of course you did,' said Art, nodding. 'Where the other gargoyles are.'

'Yes,' murmured Nancy. 'The Gargoyle Guardians.'

Arthur gave Molly an excited look. 'So we were right. They do protect the island!'

Nancy arched an elegant stone eyebrow. 'Yes, that was our most honourable role – defending our home. The gargoyles always guarded the island against attacks, ever since the building of Ravenstorm Hall. Lord Trevarren was a clever man – clever enough to feel the magic of the place, and try to harness it himself. He let magic into Ravenstorm Hall… and that was his downfall in the end. Ah, but that's a story for another day.'

Bending and twisting the pin in the lock, Molly glanced at Arthur with a smile. 'And we can't wait to hear that one!'

'He gave life to the gargoyles,' murmured Nancy, 'and they fought to protect Ravenstorm Island and its people whenever they were threatened. When war broke out two hundred years after Lord Trevarren's time, and invaders came on a submarine – oh, but I have to tell you of the pirates first.'

'Yes, *please*,' insisted Arthur.

A faraway look came into the gargoyle's lapis lazuli eyes. 'When humans came to the island, Black Edward Sharksbane knew there'd be rich pickings for his crew at Ravenstorm Hall. Over the years and the centuries he'd sail to the island now and again, robbing and thieving. His raids were sneaky, and cunning, and quick. The hall was always his target, with its treasures and beauties.

'But Sharksbane grew more ruthless. He grew stronger, and greedier, and crueller. There came a time when swiftness and sneakiness were no longer enough to satisfy him. He wanted everything the island had to give!'

'He'd got away with it for too long,' muttered Arthur, nodding sagely.

'Perhaps – and perhaps that was our fault for letting him.' Nancy's words were filled with pain and remorse. 'The next time the ghost ship came calling, the pirates stormed ashore – a great howling army of them. They raided Crowsnest, and they ransacked every house and farm – killing and destroying, seizing the possessions of even the poorest islanders.' A fierce light of rage sparked in Nancy's eyes. 'It was a merciless attack, without quarter or restraint. From the hall they stole so many valuables, so many beautiful artefacts. We tried to fight them off – we did our best, but there were so many of them. So many, and they'd taken us by surprise…

'But still he was hungry for loot, and he did not leave. The next night, when he came again with his raiders, we'd had time enough to regroup, and plan how to fight back. And Sharksbane was too sure of himself by now – he'd found Ravenstorm Island such an easy target before.

'Well, the gargoyles assembled, and this time we planned our defence more carefully. We waited till they were drunk on greed and savagery, and off their guard. We ambushed the pirates as they caroused on the village green – oh, the fear in their eyes when they saw us coming down on them!' Her smile transformed her face. 'Black Edward and his crew had never been thwarted before, and what a shock it was for them!'

'I'll bet,' murmured Molly, a hairgrip between her teeth as the mechanism gave way and the first padlock sprang open. 'Go on, Nancy. Please!'

'It was a fierce battle, and a close one. We might not have overcome them in the end, but for the fact that one of us' – Nancy's voice cracked slightly, but she recovered – 'one of us was too ambitious, too confident. The ship itself, the *Medusa* – why should we not attack that? We could sink it in the bay, destroy the pirates forever!'

There was aching regret in the gargoyle's face. 'Was it your idea, Nancy?' asked Molly softly. 'And did something go wrong?'

Nancy nodded, closing her eyes briefly in pain at the memory. 'So our leader held off Black Edward's main force, distracting them while a few of us fought our way to the *Medusa*. And as we battled, I found myself at the prow, right beneath the figurehead. A hideous thing it was, monstrous – a Gorgon with a head of snakes, and glaring red eyes, and claws for hands. And in those claws it held Black Edward's magical compass!'

Molly caught Arthur's eye, excited, but just said, 'Go on!'

'The Gorgon's compass is all that guides the pirates across the ocean wastes. There is no other that can steer them safely – the *Medusa* isn't an ordinary vessel, after all. It needs the magic of that compass, and the pirates cannot sail safely without it at their prow. But I didn't know it, not then. In my fury I tore the Gorgon from the ship, and smashed it on the rocks.'

'And it ended up in the corner of Miss B's museum!' exclaimed Arthur. 'Remember those painted eyes, Molly? It must be all that's left of the *Medusa's* figurehead.'

'The Gorgon was destroyed,' Nancy went on, her voice darkening, 'and now we came to realise the pirates would not give in. Still they fought, more fiercely than ever; it was as if a new and deadly desperation had entered them. Our forces were equally matched – and at last, in a lull in the battle, we agreed a parley.

'Black Edward's eyes – oh, I remember them, glittering with a pitiless light. He smiled like a shark as he told us the truth: that without the Gorgon and her compass to guide them, the pirates could sail no more. Black Edward and his crew would remain on Ravenstorm Island, pillaging and destroying, bringing ruin to our home forever. And we had brought this on the island, and ourselves!'

Arthur was holding his breath. 'So what did you do? What *could* you do?'

'In the darkness of that night, lit by the flames of the burning village, the gargoyles made a deal with Sharksbane.' Nancy's voice grew low and bitter. 'A deal with the devil, indeed.'

Molly bent and twisted a pin, hoping desperately that it wouldn't break – and at last the mechanism of the second padlock gave, and it snapped open. 'What happened, Nancy?'

Excitement at the memory of the battle had died altogether from Nancy's eyes, and once again they heard immense grief in her voice. 'The pirates demanded a new figurehead to hold their magical compass, to guide them across the wild ocean wastes. If the gargoyles gave them that, Black Edward said, they would leave Ravenstorm Island forever.'

Molly's hand went still on the last padlock, and she gazed up at Nancy in horror. 'You!' she whispered. 'They handed you over to be the new figurehead…'

Nancy gave a brief nod. 'I destroyed the Gorgon; I captured the compass. The plan to attack the ship was mine. The pirates wanted vengeance, and my friends believed they had no choice, for the island's sake. They gave me over to Black Edward.'

Arthur breathed an angry sigh. 'That's terrible. How could they? There had to be another way!'

Nancy was silent for a long moment, as if remembering. Then she nodded again, abruptly. 'Yes. Yes, I think there must have been another way, but they didn't take time to think of it. They were too afraid.'

'Too cowardly!' said Arthur.

'Yes. Perhaps. But I was handed over to Black Edward, and I've been at his mercy ever since. His, and his ghastly crew's.' She laughed bitterly. 'How they've loved having me as their slave. Bound to this ship, sailing on forever into freezing seas and howling weather, and watching them ravage other islands, other homes. They appear to human ships sometimes, hoping to scare them into losing control and sinking. Oh, it was a grand victory the gargoyles won.'

'You must have been so angry,' murmured Molly as the first chain rattled loose from Nancy's arm. She caught it quickly, cross with herself and hoping the pirate guards hadn't heard. 'It was you that cursed the gargoyles, wasn't it?'

'I did. I doomed them to be stone forever, and I cursed their leader never to leave the bounds of Ravenstorm Hall.'

'I don't blame you,' said Arthur fiercely. 'I'd have cursed them a *lot* worse.'

Nancy shook her head, and extended her one free arm, showing them her palm. The stony flesh was badly cracked, with jagged scars where chips of it had fallen away.

'I never wanted to lead Black Edward to other poor towns, guide him to his loot. Years it took me, but at last I tore the compass from my hand. I threw it into the waves in a storm, and I hoped it was lost forever.'

'But it wasn't,' breathed Arthur. 'We found it, washed up on the shore. Remember, Molly? What Charley said about the strange currents? They must have drawn it here.'

'I feared as much,' sighed Nancy. 'The compass would not be so easily destroyed. And where the compass goes, the pirate ship follows. They cannot be separated, not ever, and so Black Edward has returned to Ravenstorm Island at last. And without his magical guide, he will never leave again. He will take his revenge on the island, and on the gargoyles who set a troublemaker on their ship.'

Arthur tugged at a chain, loosening it so that Molly could pick more easily at the final padlock. 'Well, the gargoyles deserve whatever they get,' he whispered savagely. 'But the island doesn't.'

'That's true.' Nancy shook her head, sorrowful. 'I'm sorry I ever flung the compass overboard, if it means my home is threatened once again.'

'It doesn't have to mean that.' Molly twisted the pin, and the padlock gave. She stepped back and gazed fiercely at Nancy. 'This is your chance to go back to your home, and protect it.'

She slipped the lock's hasp out of the chain, and the rusty links slithered clear into her waiting arms.

With a breathless gasp of joy, Nancy leaped lightly down from the post that had held her captive for so long. Her feet touched the deck with astonishing lightness and she spun around, her storm-tattered, stone-coloured silken dress swirling around her. Her hair swung loose and wild in the wind, the enchanted rays of the lighthouse turning its coppery glint to silver.

'Home!' She stretched her arms towards the sky, her face split in a smile of pure delight. 'Home, and free at last!'

'Thank you, Molly and Arthur. Oh, thank you!' Nancy seized each of their hands and spun them around too. 'But how did you come here? Why did you board this terrible ship?'

Molly gave a start. Of course – in the excitement of finding and freeing Nancy, she'd forgotten for a moment why they were there. Her heart sank. 'Oh, Nancy,' she whispered. 'You're not their only prisoner. The pirates kidnapped a friend of ours – she's—'

Nancy lifted a slender hand. 'I know who you mean, and I know exactly where she is. I saw them bring her on board. Follow me, and we'll free your friend as well.'

Putting a finger to her lips, she caught up her skirts in one arm and crept across the decks, keeping the main mast and the rigging between them and the pirate guards, who were now guffawing loudly as they shared tots from a rum barrel on the quarterdeck.

'They'll be in big trouble with their captain later,' murmured Nancy with a wink, as she crouched with the cousins behind a pile of crates. 'Not that I care two hoots! But look – you see the hatch just beyond them? That's the way to the brig, and the brig's where they'll have put the old lady.'

'That's tricky, then.' Arthur frowned. 'Those great thuggish lumps are between us and Miss Badcrumble.'

Molly shut one eye, studying the play of the silver lighthouse beam and thinking hard. 'Tricky…that's exactly the word.'

Arthur glanced at her in amusement. 'You always have a plan, Molly Cornell. Which trick this time?'

Molly grinned at her cousin and whispered, 'Look at the shadows. Can't you just imagine how scary Black Edward Sharksbane would be, looming through them?'

Sure enough, the combination of Miss Badcrumble's magical fix of the lighthouse beam and the eerie intermittent moonlight cast high leaping shadows across the whole ship. They were such a contrast, and so distorted, they looked downright ominous – at least, they did if you didn't know what was casting them. The shadow of the rigging, for instance: that looked like the ghastly web of a monster spider.

Arthur put a hand on Molly's arm. 'I think I get it!' he muttered excitedly.

Quickly, Molly pulled out some elastic hair bands from her pocket, wrapping them round her fingers.

Arthur grinned at her, switching his gaze to the gargoyle. 'Nancy – Molly's got a great idea. Can she, er…do something to your hair?'

Molly was delighted Arthur knew what she was thinking. She began weaving three braids of Nancy's flowing red hair, and when she finished she whispered urgently into her ear. Nancy's face broke into a broad smile as she clambered onto one of the crates and the cousins leaned at her sides, the three of them making one gigantic shadow.

'HO!' shouted Arthur in a thunderously deep voice.

The guards leaped up so suddenly, the rum barrel tumbled over and one of them went sprawling. The bald pirate with the hoop earring whisked his cutlass from its sheath and brandished it, blinking against the brilliant light.

'Who the devil goes there?' he yelled, but Molly noticed his voice was shaking.

And so it should, she thought, barely able to suppress a giggle. The huge shadow cast across the deck looked like a burly terrifying man, three plaits sticking out from his head.

I've never actually been *a shadow puppet before*, she thought.

'Is that you, Cap'n?' The pirate's voice was suddenly suspicious.

But Arthur rose to the challenge. 'AYE! Scurvy useless dogs! At my rum, are ye?'

Still squinting, but clearly more nervous now, the pirate took a step back. 'Cap'n, I…'

'GET TO WORK!' roared Arthur. 'Shirking yer duties, are ye? Get that poop deck scrubbed or I'll KEEL-HAUL THE THREE OF YIS.'

The bald pirate might have said something more, but the scrawny pair with him had heard enough. Grabbing him, they staggered back from the shadow, and suddenly they were all running to obey, falling over one another in their eagerness to be away from their captain's wrath.

Molly hugged herself in delight, then hugged Arthur too. 'You're an amazing mimic!'

'There's no end to my talents,' agreed Arthur with a solemn wink.

'It won't work for long,' warned Nancy, jumping down from the crate and putting a hand on each of their shoulders. 'Let's go and find your friend!'

The hatch over the brig looked solid and heavy, but Nancy hauled it up with ease, then held it while Molly and Art clambered down the damp and slippery ladder into the darkness below. Molly heard her follow them, the hatch creaking softly shut behind her. When it closed again, the blackness was complete, and it seemed suddenly far colder. Molly shivered.

There was a dripping sound that echoed dully, and the air smelt of salt and mould and fish. Disoriented, Molly reached out a hand and touched wet planks. An icy sensation trickled up her fingers, and she remembered once again that this was a ghost ship.

'Can you see, Art?' she whispered, and promptly wished she hadn't. The sound of her own voice in the darkness was disembodied and eerie.

'I'm starting to,' came her cousin's response. 'There's a sort of glow. Hang on.'

Molly blinked and realised he was right. There *was* a faint ghostly light; whether it came from the dank pools of seawater sloshing across the planks, or from the ship itself, Molly neither knew nor cared. Now that her eyes were adjusting she could make out bulkheads and dim corners, and stacks of barrels and rope. And there, further down the passageway, she caught the rusty glint of metal bars.

As she and Arthur fumbled their way towards the cell, with Nancy behind them, a pair of spindly birdlike claws came forward to grip the bars. Suddenly Miss Badcrumble's pale face loomed from the darkness, framed by her frizzy grey hair, her eyes wide and terrified.

'Molly! Arthur! What are you doing here?'

'Rescuing you, of course,' said Arthur firmly. He laid a hand on Miss Badcrumble's.

'But you can't! Oh dear. It's too dangerous. Oh dear.' Miss Badcrumble sounded on the verge of panicked tears.

'Don't be silly,' said Arthur. 'We'll have you out of there in no time.'

'Where are the keys?' Molly asked the old Sprye urgently. 'Do you know where they're kept?' She felt her own surge of fear as she realised they hadn't bargained on this. How were they going to break Miss Badcrumble free if they couldn't find the key?

The lock was a big solid metal one; no padlocks here that were pickable with a little hairgrip.

'We won't need a key,' came Nancy's confident voice.

Miss Badcrumble gave a muffled shriek and clapped her hands over her mouth. 'Who's that?'

'This is Nancy, and she's a friend of ours,' Arthur told her. 'Which means she's a friend of *yours*. Oh yes, and she's a gargoyle.'

'Oh my,' said Miss Badcrumble faintly.

'The ship's spell over me is breaking,' Nancy told them. 'I've been weakened by the *Medusa* for a long time, but I'm not chained to her now. My strength is coming back. Stand away. And you, Miss Badcrumble.'

Molly pulled Arthur back as Nancy stepped forward and seized a bar in each hand. The stony muscles in her back and shoulders flexed and stretched, and then she was wrenching the bars slowly apart. Molly gazed in awe as flakes of rust fell to the ground, the squeal of tortured metal filling the dank air as the bars bent slowly in

Nancy's remorseless hands.

Letting one bar go, Nancy wrapped both hands round the other, jammed her feet against the wall, and twisted hard, her teeth gritted. With a sudden shriek and clang, the bar gave at last. It tore out of its socket and Nancy flung it aside, then dusted her hands together in satisfaction.

'Wow,' murmured Molly. She held her breath and gazed up towards the deck, wishing she could see through it to be sure the pirates hadn't heard. But perhaps the guards were still too afraid of their captain's wrath, and were hard at work swabbing.

Arthur was reaching for Miss Badcrumble, helping her step tentatively through the yawning gap. As soon as the old Sprye had tugged her skirts free, she hopped clear and flung herself at Molly and Art, hugging them tightly. Molly brushed the old woman's hair out of her eyes and returned her hug.

'We're not out of here yet,' she reminded the others. 'Let's go before the guards realise their captain isn't around after all.'

'I couldn't agree more,' said Nancy, and led them back to the ladder, going ahead this time to lift the hatch cautiously with her strong shoulders. She peered out through the slit, then shoved it wide. 'Come on! Let's not waste time.'

Molly climbed out first, then reached down to help Miss Badcrumble, picking her way awkwardly up the creaking ladder as she tried to keep her long skirts from tangling around her ankles. Then Nancy kept watch as Arthur climbed out last.

'Quick!' whispered Arthur. 'Our boat's under the stern.'

As silently as they could they crept back along the decks. Molly could feel her heart pounding painfully in her ribcage as they passed close by the muttering pirate guards, now on their knees and scrubbing at the decks as they complained in gruff undertones about the stress of the sailor's life.

'Have a ship of me own, one day, I will,' grumbled Gold-Hoop. 'Somebody else can do the scrubbin'.'

'Shut yer mouth or the cap'n'll hear ye!'

'Both of yis are hurtin' my ears,' growled the third. 'Save yer breath! I'm doin' all the work here.'

With all their moaning, it was no wonder they hadn't heard the noise of the two escapes. Arthur looked over his shoulder and gave Molly a grin, but Molly was too anxious to return it. It would take just one slip, and then the guards would be onto them. And no shadow-puppet would fool them this time...

Arthur's rope still dangled from the rail, and one by one they hauled themselves over the edge and lowered themselves down. Nancy went ahead of Miss Badcrumble, helping her fumble her way down the rope and ignoring her tiny squeals of terror whenever her grip loosened. Agonising minutes passed before they were all in the cabin of Charley's boat and Arthur was unfastening the rope and letting it fall to the deck.

Molly noticed that her cousin was holding his breath as he tentatively fired the ignition, but there was still no sign of movement from the pirates up above, no sound of an alarm or the furious shouts of tricked thugs. Keeping the engine at an easy low idle, Arthur steered the boat quietly out from under the stern and into open water. Not until they were a good hundred metres from the pirate ship did he risk turning up the power and the speed.

Eagerly peering towards the shore, barely daring to believe they'd got away from the *Medusa* without being discovered, Molly felt a cold hand slip into hers. Nancy, she realised, glancing up with a smile at the beautiful gargoyle. Her hand felt less like stone than Molly had expected; the skin was softer and warmer the closer they came to shore, and there were tears shining in her blue eyes.

'I can't believe I'm really going home,' whispered Nancy.

Molly squeezed her hand. The gargoyle's touch reminded her of how the children turned to statues by the Queen of the Shadowsprye had slowly warmed into true, breathing life when the spell was broken. Not only was Nancy becoming real, and warm, and human; her wings were shrinking into her shoulder blades. Even as Molly watched, spellbound, they shrivelled and dwindled and were absorbed into Nancy's back.

She didn't look the least bit monstrous; indeed her transformation reminded Molly strongly of someone else besides Shadowsprye statues.

'You're more like Mason than the other gargoyles,' she blurted. 'You look more…sort of…human.'

Nancy looked a little alarmed, a little uncomfortable, but she said nothing. Unable to ignore her curiosity, Molly tugged her around and faced her.

'Why is that? Why aren't you like the stone gargoyles?'

Nancy turned swiftly away and back towards the line of white waves breaking against the island shore. 'It doesn't matter. Look, we're there. I'm really, truly home!'

Arthur brought Charley's boat in against the jetty, where it bumped and rocked against the line of tyres. The wind howled and whirled, snatching at Molly's hair and dashing her face with cold rain as she jumped out to catch the painter and loop it securely around the bollards.

'No sign or sound of the pirates,' remarked Arthur as he helped Miss Badcrumble over the gunwale and onto dry land, 'but I doubt very much they've gone back to their ship.'

'I'm sure they haven't.' Molly shivered. 'The weather's still raging, isn't it? They're probably off raiding one of the farms, or the big houses on the other side of the island. I bet we hear of storm damage tomorrow.'

'We'll see about that,' said Nancy grimly. 'Now, I've got some work to do before we deal with these raiders.'

Needing no helping hand, she sprang lightly up onto the jetty. She already seemed even taller than before, and she radiated happiness. As she determinedly clenched and unclenched her fists, Molly noticed that her fingernails were very long and smooth, with a hard polish like semi-precious stones. They made her look even more fierce and dangerous, and Molly was glad the beautiful gargoyle was on their side.

Let's see Black Edward handle Nancy when she isn't in chains! she thought, pride at their new friend swelling in her throat.

Molly couldn't help but smile as the gargoyle strode down the jetty and leaped onto the beach. As soon as Nancy's feet touched the sand she crouched down, burying her long fingers in it, a smile of pure joy lighting her features. She didn't look even remotely like a gargoyle now, thought Molly: she had a flinty, graceful loveliness.

'What's she doing?' hissed Arthur at Molly's elbow.

Tilting her head and listening, Molly watched along with the other two. Sure enough, Nancy had closed her eyes and was chanting something soft and rhythmic, over and over again.

'If you ask me, dears,' murmured Miss Badcrumble, 'I'd say she was casting a spell.'

'Or undoing one?' Molly held her breath. 'I think she's lifting the curse, Arthur!'

'I'm sure you're right.' Art grinned. 'She's so happy to be back. I didn't think she could go on being so angry!'

The night seemed very still suddenly, and Molly realised the wind had dropped. Though clouds scudded high above them, and the silhouettes of the furthest trees still tossed in a storm, there seemed to be a bubble of calm where they stood. Molly found she was holding her breath again, as if afraid to disturb it.

Something moved above the trees on the crest of the island: dark shapes that Molly thought for a moment were just scraps of stormcloud. As they drew closer she could make out distinct flying forms: too big to be bats or birds, and growing bigger by the second. Moments later, the sky was full of them, clawed and winged, leathery creatures with grotesque tusked faces – some birdlike, some reptilian, and some almost human. They circled and soared, swooping down and making Miss Badcrumble duck with a frightened squeak, her skinny hands over her head.

'I know those!' cried Arthur with delight as one swept past him, wings flapping. 'They're the gargoyles. From Ravenstorm Hall!'

The night was suddenly a tumult of gargoyles, crying and mewling like hoarse gulls or high-pitched crows: Molly couldn't decide which. She gazed around in wonder, feeling the air being churned by their speed as they spun in a great flock around them, then settled one by one and folded their wings. One landed on the broken roof of Charley's cottage, one on her fence. Two landed on the sea wall, gripping it with their great claws and catching their balance with their wings. All of them stretched and flexed their muscles, shaking themselves, kneading the ground like great cats or extending a leathery wing and preening it with their claws. Their eyes were wide and round and darkest purple, set in those extraordinary faces – so ugly they were almost beautiful.

One of the gargoyles landed elegantly right in front of Nancy, folded its wings and raised a clawed foreleg to her. As it gazed up with those violet-marble eyes, Molly felt a lump in her throat. The creature looked as if it was asking Nancy for something: something only Nancy could give.

Nancy bent to it – it reached no higher than her knees – and laid a hand on its scaly head, then stroked its neck and murmured to it. Still it went on gazing at her, giving small joyful cries like a bird. For long minutes the gargoyles continued to land, creeping and hopping and scuttling closer to Nancy, until the whole great cloud of them were earthbound and surrounding her, every eye riveted on her smiling face, their heads tilted with adoration.

'I've never seen anything like it,' whispered Arthur.

'Well, that's not surprising,' Molly whispered back with a grin – even though she felt tears pricking her eyes. 'We've just watched a flock of enchanted gargoyles come to life.'

'Eighteen of them.' Arthur gazed in wonder. 'I think that's all. There are eighteen gargoyles on Ravenstorm Hall.'

'Nineteen.' Nancy rose, and gazed at them both. 'Not quite all of them are here. There's one missing.'

Arthur exchanged an apprehensive glance with Molly.

'Nancy. Do you mean—'

'Would you take me to the hall now?' Nancy stood up straight, looking stern and beautiful in the centre of her worshipful flock of gargoyles. 'Will you take me home to see Mason?'

It was a strange and almost-unreal walk back to the gates of the hall, the sky above them thick with flying gargoyles and the air full of the beating of those leathery wings. Between scudding clouds, the moonlight gleamed on scaly hides and glinted off sharp claws. Molly couldn't help but glance up frequently in wonder.

If I never see magic again, she thought, *at least I'll know that I once saw a flight of gargoyles. And I've never seen anything more magnificent...*

'What will the villagers think if they see them?' she muttered to Arthur at one point, but Miss Badcrumble was right behind them, ready to reassure.

'Don't worry, my dears,' said the old Sprye. 'They're like the ghosts. You can only see them because of your protective charms. If any of the islanders pass by, they'll only feel a stiff breeze. They might shiver a little, I suppose, if they felt a wingtip brush their cheek…'

Arthur nudged Molly. 'I'm sure that's happened to me before, even on the mainland,' he whispered. 'Maybe magic doesn't only happen on Ravenstorm Island after all.'

The night was not entirely dark; on the horizon there was the first pearly suggestion of dawn, and as they rounded the end of the lane they saw the gateposts of Ravenstorm Hall rearing up, impressive against the navy-blue and charcoal of the sky. There was another shadow too, visible through the wrought iron gates: a tall figure with broad square shoulders. Molly hesitated, nervously adjusting her backpack straps. For a moment she thought Mason might be waiting to tick them off again for yet another midnight expedition, but she realised she needn't have worried. As they all walked closer his features became clear.

His stern face was full of wonder, and he was looking not at her and Arthur at all, but at Nancy. The tall and beautiful redhead came to a halt as he walked slowly, uncertainly forward and gripped the bars of the gates.

'Nancy?' His gruff voice trembled. '*Nancy*. Is it really you?'

Molly pulled Arthur's arm and hung back, watching the two huge gargoyles as Nancy approached the iron gates. Mason looked even more shocked than he had at the sight of the ship's compass. His greyish skin was paler than ever and she thought she could glimpse the shine of tears in his eyes.

'You know, I think they were in love once,' murmured Molly.

Arthur whispered, 'I think they still are.'

Nancy hadn't spoken, but she stepped close to the gates and watched Mason through the bars. Her hands shook slightly, and she clenched them tightly at her sides.

'Nancy,' he whispered. 'I knew it must be you. I knew you must be back. When the gargoyles came back to life, and took flight…'

He glanced up, watching them swoop and circle, uttering their harsh cries of happiness. Molly saw his chest heave with a great sigh; then he looked back at Nancy, his eyes full of sorrow.

'Nancy. I'm so sorry. I should never have let them—'

'Hush.' Nancy came forward and touched his hands with her own. 'That's all you had to say.'

'I could have found another way. I could have stopped them giving you to Sharksbane. I should have fought them all with my bare hands, Nancy. I've never regretted anything so much in my—'

To silence him, Nancy leaned forward and kissed him gently on his hard lips. As she drew away she smiled and squeezed his hands. 'I mean it, Mason. You don't have to say any more.'

He blinked, and smiled. Beside Molly, Arthur

scratched at the corner of his eye.

'Honestly, Moll, I could get quite sentimental,' he whispered.

'You're not the only one.' Molly smiled. Just behind Arthur, Miss Badcrumble was snuffling into her voluminous sleeve.

Mason reached for the latch on the gate, but Nancy caught his hand to stop him. 'No need for that,' she smiled. Closing her eyes, she tipped her head back.

Though there seemed to be hardly any breeze now, her hair was caught by some invisible gust, billowing out behind her. Her hands over Mason's curled and lengthened, the gleaming nails stretching into curved claws; her skin looked for a moment as if it was icing over, till Molly realised it was simply hardening into grey stone. Yet Nancy and Mason were so much bigger than the other gargoyles, and so much more human as well.

Mason's fingers, too, were lengthening into talons; they looked remarkably gentle resting against

Nancy's. His skin grew dark and scaly, and as bat-like wings sprouted and stretched from his back, a tail grew, too, long and scaled and powerful. As it stretched out to its full length he lashed it triumphantly back and forth.

Nancy's black-feathered wings were growing far huger than they had been before; she flexed and extended them like dark angel. Between her wings and Mason's, the sky was momentarily blotted out.

Molly and Arthur gazed at the pair's transformation, enchanted. 'Nancy's so different,' Arthur whispered. 'As if she was only half her true form on the ship.'

'I guess this is how she's meant to be,' Molly whispered back. 'She's beautiful.'

'So's Mason, in a scary way.'

Indeed they both were, thought Molly: frightening and beautiful and altogether awe-inspiring. Drawn up now to their full heights, they scraped and clawed at the ground, scoring great lines in the drive on either side of the gate. Roaring, Mason reared back on his hind claws and suddenly he was airborne, and soaring skywards. When he dived, it was straight towards Nancy on the other side of the gate. With a cry of joy, she flew up to join him.

'Mason can leave Ravenstorm Hall!' shouted Arthur, his eyes shining. 'Nancy really has lifted the curse!'

Sure enough, the two huge gargoyles were flying in circles above them, well beyond the boundaries of the hall. The smaller gargoyles flew to meet them, swarming in a melee around and below, never once colliding or even touching wingtips. The sky was full of their harsh mewling noises.

Mason soared in a wide circle to touch down right in front of the gawping cousins and Miss Badcrumble. Glancing first at his right wing, then at his left, he smiled; Molly thought his stern face was entirely transformed.

'And now we can defend our home again, as Lord Trevarren intended. We were his faithful servants, but we were nearly killed when part of the hall collapsed on us. He saved our lives by transforming us into the creatures you see before you, and in our gratitude we swore to always protect Ravenstorm Island.' Mason's voice echoed in the night as Nancy landed gracefully at his side.

Molly grinned at Arthur. *So that's why they both look so beautifully, scarily different from the other gargoyles – they were human once!*

'It's all thanks to you two, Master Arthur, Molly. You've freed Nancy, and now she has freed us too.' Flinging out his arms, Mason summoned the army of gargoyles, and they hovered and swooped above him in a clatter of wings. Molly felt the breeze of them on her face, and her hair blustered and tangled.

Above the noise, Mason called again. 'It's time to fight, my friends! It's time to save Ravenstorm Island from Sharksbane once again. Who's with me?'

There was a clamour of shrieks and howls as Nancy linked her taloned hands with Mason's and they smiled at one another. Together they sprang up into the air once more.

'Hey, wait a minute!' Arthur's yell made them stop and hover, and glance back down.

'Master Arthur?'

'Don't think you're going without us! Right, Molly?'

'Right!' called Molly. 'We're coming too.'

'And so am I!' Miss Badcrumble blushed at her own daring, but there was a light of excitement in her crinkled eyes.

'Master Arthur, I'm not sure your parents...'

Art glowered at him, hands on his hips. 'Mason, we climbed aboard the *Medusa* all by ourselves and rescued Nancy.'

'That's right,' Molly said. 'We are *not* being left behind just when things get interesting.'

With a grin at Nancy, Mason flexed his huge wings and flapped down to the ground again. 'Very well. I daresay you've earned the right to come with us.'

'They certainly have.' Nancy landed elegantly next to Art and reached out a hand to help him climb up onto her back.

Molly reached for Mason's claws and let him pull her up onto his scaly back; then she turned and between them they helped Miss Badcrumble up behind her. The old Sprye's hands gripped her waist tightly.

'Oh, Molly, dear! This is *terribly* exciting but maybe it's not such a good ideEEEEA!'

Miss Badcrumble's squeal of alarm was whipped back into her throat as Mason soared up and wheeled into the night. The old woman buried her face in Molly's shoulder blades and the grip of her slender bird-claws on Molly's waist was stronger than she could ever have predicted.

Molly gasped, barely able to catch her breath. Night wind rushed past her ears and her head was full of the strong pulse of beating gargoyle-wings. They filled the air around her. Not far away she could see Arthur, gripping Nancy's shoulders for dear life, but there was a grin of delight plastered on her cousin's face.

'Look, Molly. Look!'

Don't look down – wasn't that the advice people always gave? All the same Molly dared to do it, and she was instantly thrilled. The treetops of Ravenstorm Hall were already tiny beneath them, their spiky crowns gilded with moonlight, and the turrets and spires of the hall itself were like a fairytale castle far below. Turning, she could see the whole island, its dark shores outlined in foaming silver surf, and the black sea seemed to stretch forever in a vast three-hundred-and-sixty degree circle. Her heart beat with wild excitement even as she felt the first cold spatters of rain on her face.

As they hurtled through the night away from the hall, the rain intensified, and in seconds it was lashing Molly's face, the storm howling in her ears. It didn't matter. No longer able to hear Arthur's shouts of elation, she gave an ecstatic whoop herself that was snatched away by the wind. Miss Badcrumble was still clutching her tightly, but she had taken her face away from Molly's back and was gazing down in awe at the island spread out below.

'Ooh!' the old Sprye cried. 'I've always wondered how it felt to be a *flying* Sprye.'

Mason's commands echoed through the storm, drowning out Miss Badcrumble's squeaks. 'Find Sharksbane and his crew! Brother Stonebeak, search the coast. Sister Pebblehide, south of the village. Sister Graniteguts – the north!'

His troops soared off in disciplined detachments to scour the countryside, returning now and then with news that they conveyed to Mason in urgent yips and howls. Fast as the small gargoyles flew, Molly's heart was in her throat. What mayhem could Black Edward and his gang be causing even now?

For what seemed far too long – but must have been less than two minutes – the leathery creatures swooped back and forth, quartering the island. At last a black-feathered gargoyle with a twisted raven's beak fluttered before Mason, its shriek filled with fevered importance. Mason flapped his great wings, hovering, then glanced back over his shoulder at Molly.

'Found them!' he shouted, then turned back to call to the others. 'Sharksbane is in the Main Street of Crowsnest! To me!'

Molly felt wind rush across her face as he shot ahead of the rest, Nancy at his side with Arthur crouched low over her back. As the street lights of Crowsnest blinked into view, strung like a delicate necklace across the bay, Miss Badcrumble pointed over Molly's shoulder and gave a cry.

'They're ransacking my lovely museum again!'

Sure enough, Molly could see a gang of pirates around Miss Badcrumble's little home: smashing windows, wrenching slates from the roof and flinging them down to the pavement to shatter. One hairy pirate swung a branch wildly above his head, about to slam it into the door, but as he tilted his head back and glimpsed what was above him, he gave a yell of alarm.

Mason spun upwards. Molly gasped and clung on tight to his back as he turned, then dived like a falcon, the other gargoyles in formation behind him. As the wind streamed through Molly's hair and Miss Badcrumble squeezed her arms tighter, Molly saw the glint of light on sabres and cutlasses, and she made out the unmistakeable figure of Edward Sharksbane, pointing to the sky as he yelled in fury.

'We're attacked! Fight 'em, comrades!'

The pirates drew their blades, hollering and screaming up at the attackers. Mason swooped past Sharksbane in a perilous feinting movement, and the pirate captain gave a shriek of rage.

'The old woman! By the bones of my grandfather, she'll tell us yet where the compass is! You hear me, crone? I'll tear this place apart if I have to!'

Mason, grim-faced, did not answer, but Arthur yelled from Nancy's back.

'That compass isn't all you've lost, you ugly thief!'

Snarling, Sharksbane swivelled his mutilated face towards him – and that was when he laid eyes on Nancy.

'You!'

'Lost your figurehead, too!' shouted Arthur as

Nancy dipped and swooped, her wingtip slashing across the captain's face.

Sharksbane paled, looking demented with rage, as he shook his cutlass at the retreating gargoyle woman.

'She's free – the red-haired witch is free! Kill them! Kill them *all*!'

'You can try,' shouted Nancy, a savage grin on her face as she turned and swooped.

'If you're hard enough,' added Arthur, with a hoot of derision.

Mason dived again, and suddenly the battle exploded around Molly as lightning crackled above. Deafened by screams and yells and the clash of blades and claws and teeth, half-blinded by rain, she gripped tightly onto Mason's back. The smaller gargoyles were in among the pirate gang now, scratching and biting and dodging the shining blades as they hacked and lashed.

Molly gasped in alarm as a massive, black-bearded pirate caught a gargoyle's flank with his heavy staff, sending it tumbling out of control towards a wall. For a ghastly moment, as the pirate grinned and advanced on the creature, Molly yelled a horrified warning – how could it escape the second lethal strike? But the frog-faced gargoyle twisted quickly and shot skywards as the pirate screamed a curse. It seemed the gargoyles, for all that they looked so squat and clumsy, were incredibly nimble in the air.

I have to stop worrying and let them get on with it! Molly berated herself. Besides, she had to concentrate on keeping her own head down, ducking and dodging as Mason twisted and flew through the gang, flailing his tail and swiping with his claws. One blow of his scaly tail caught a tall pirate in the belly and sent him slamming into a tree; leaves fluttered down around the man's stunned head.

She couldn't leave all this to Mason and Nancy and their gargoyle friends – after all, hadn't she and Arthur asked to be taken along? Molly set her teeth. The pirate who had been about to smash Miss Badcrumble's door dropped his branch as the gargoyles attacked, so the next time Mason sailed low to the ground Molly snatched it up.

A tusked gargoyle was struggling with a burly pirate; Molly took her chance. Swinging the branch as Mason sailed past, she whacked it hard into the pirate's back and he fell flat on his face. Flapping up and away from him, the gargoyle gave her a grateful squeal and turned to deal with another member of the gang.

As Mason turned elegantly in the air, slapping a pirate to the ground with one well-aimed wing, Molly saw a skinny raider lunge for Arthur, trying to drag him from Nancy's back. And Nancy was too distracted to help, struggling in fierce claw-to-hand combat with an enraged woman pirate...

'Mason!' cried Molly. 'Mason, Art's in trouble!'

Mason spun on a wingtip, ready to defend a son of Ravenstorm Hall – but at that moment Arthur gave his attacker a well-aimed kick right in the solar plexus, and he slumped to the ground, clutching his stomach, winded. Nancy, her own opponent now sprawled face-down in the grass, took her chance to seize Arthur's stunned attacker by the leg, whirl him round her head, and spin him away like an Olympic hammer.

Mason gave her a shout of appreciation. 'It's like old times, Nancy!'

'That it is, my love.' Her smile was sweet as her fist cracked into another enemy's nose.

The pirate crew had met their match, thought Molly with satisfaction; but she couldn't help feeling a niggling worry at the same time. Just like old times it might be – but from the way Mason and Nancy talked, it seemed that those 'old times' had happened more often than was good for Ravenstorm Island. A satisfying scrap was all very well – but if the pirates couldn't be defeated once and for all, what was to stop them returning again and again to Ravenstorm Island?

And after Nancy's escape, and the loss of their precious compass, they would be even more vengeful and bitter than before…

Behind her Miss Badcrumble gave a gasp of annoyance, and Molly turned in time to see her stretch out her long skinny arm towards the three ghostly men tearing at the museum's window shutters. A bolt of pink energy crackled from the old woman's claw-tips, racing like wildfire into the ivy that crept up the wall. Flickering with cold flame, the plant tore away from its anchorage and coiled round the pirates, looping and tightening and hauling them upwards till they were suspended helpless in its tendrils.

'Way to go, Miss B!' shouted Molly in delight as she watched the dangling raiders kick and struggle in futile rage. The twisting, coiling ivy was like the tentacles of a giant octopus, and they had just as much chance of escaping it. They wriggled and swore and squirmed, but the ivy wasn't letting go. Despite the peril of the situation, Molly had to put a hand over her mouth to stifle a giggle.

'That'll teach them to scratch my woodwork,' said Miss Badcrumble firmly.

Molly's helpless laughter turned into a thoughtful frown as she glanced back at Miss Badcrumble again. 'Yes, it will,' she said. 'And you've just given me an idea, too. That ivy...you brought it to life! How strong are your spells?'

'Why, they can be quite powerful,' said Miss Badcrumble modestly. 'Not anything like the Queen's spells, you know, but still...'

Molly leaned forward, tugging at the edge of Mason's leathery wing. 'Mason,' she yelled over the racket of battle. 'Mason, can you take us to Charley's cottage?'

'Molly, my dear,' began Miss Badcrumble. 'Are you sure this is quite the time to—'

Mason slapped another raider to the ground and frowned back at them both. 'Now, Molly?'

'Yes – I mean – I've got an idea, Mason! Please – it's to do with the *Medusa*. I think it might work. You need to get me and Miss Badcrumble back to Starfish Cottage.'

'Me, dear?' asked Miss Badcrumble, bewildered.

'I don't like to leave Nancy,' growled Mason. 'Or the others.' He flapped into the air, watching the fight go on around them. For the moment the gargoyles had the upper hand, but although the pirates had been taken well and truly by surprise, they were fighting back.

'Do you think Nancy and Arthur could drive the pirates back to their ship?' asked Molly. 'If they could just do that…'

'We have the advantage for now.' Mason nodded. 'Though I'm not sure how long that will last. Edward Sharksbane is no mean foe.'

'Neither is Nancy,' said Molly firmly.

'Indeed.' Mason gave a laugh of delight. 'Nancy, my love!' he called.

As the red-haired gargoyle swooped closer, he extended a wingtip to touch hers. 'Can you hold them off, Nancy, as I once did for you?'

'But this time,' called Molly, 'instead of just beating the pirates, can you herd them back to their ship?'

Nancy frowned in puzzlement, then a smile

transformed her face. 'If you ask it, Molly, I can do it. I trust you, child!' And she soared back into battle, diving straight for Black Edward with a shriek of challenge.

'Oh, my,' blustered Miss Badcrumble. 'Will she – will they – will we—'

'I know Nancy can do as you ask, Molly,' said Mason with a frown of concern. 'But what's your idea? This did not end well for us before.'

'I'll explain as we go. This time I think it'll end differently. If I've got this right, Mason, the ghost pirates will never return to Ravenstorm Island again.'

He gave her a smile over his scaly shoulder. 'Then that has to be worth a try, young lady. To Starfish Cottage it is!'

The clatter and shriek of the whirling storm and the bitter struggle still echoed behind them as Mason flew gracefully over Starfish Cottage, then circled to land on the lawn, his claws raking furrows in the rough grass. He had barely touched down when Molly jumped from his back and ran through the cold slanting drizzle to the piles of rubble the raiders had left behind, after wreaking their destruction on Charley's property. Her legs felt shaky from the rollercoaster ride through the sky on Mason's back, but she adjusted quickly.

Behind her, Mason was helping Miss Badcrumble down from his back; she leaned heavily on his scaly hand, then slid and stumbled down with a small gasp of fright. Straightening up, she dusted down her skirts, smoothed her hopelessly frizzed hair, then, her dignity restored a little, she hobbled over the piles of rubbish to Molly's side. Mason was keeping an alert lookout for the approach of any pirates.

'I know it's here somewhere,' muttered Molly, throwing aside bits of slate and brick and sodden, splintered wood. Desperately she wiped rain from her eyes.

'What are you looking for, my dear?' Miss Badcrumble peered inquisitively over her shoulder. 'Can I help?'

'No, it's – ah!' Molly gave a grin of triumph as she retrieved the old squid door knocker from the rubble. She brandished it happily.

'Good heavens.' Miss Badcrumble peered at it doubtfully. 'What a...er, what an eccentric, er... accessory.'

'But useful, I hope.' Molly rubbed brick dust off the squid's tentacles, biting her lip. 'It was your trick with the ivy, Miss Badcrumble, putting a spell on it and bringing it to life. It gave me an idea. Could you do the same to this?'

'Oh, dear.' Miss Badcrumble stared down at the door knocker. 'Yes, I could, but I think – I mean, it's an extraordinary little thing, but I – don't – I don't really see what that could do for us,' she finished lamely.

'Well, first we need it to be bigger.' Anxious about the time they were wasting, Molly stretched out her arms wide to demonstrate. 'About as big as Nancy?'

Understanding brightened the old Sprye's face as if a bulb had clicked on.

'Oh! I see, I see!' Miss Badcrumble's eyes gleamed, and for a moment her smile was full of real Shadowsprye malice. 'As big as Nancy – or that horrid old Gorgon, eh? I believe I know just what you're thinking!'

Molly slipped her backpack from her shoulders, undid the straps and rummaged inside. 'Would this help? I know it's magical.' Drawing out Edward

Sharksbane's treasured compass, she displayed it on the palm of her hand.

Miss Badcrumble, though, shook her head. 'No need for that dreadful thing, my dear. I have magic of my own, and it's a good deal stronger than Sharksbane's toy. Now, step back, Molly. A little distance would be safer.'

Hurriedly Molly backed against Mason's powerful sides, and he dipped a huge wing protectively over her. Both of them peered with fascination at Miss Badcrumble as she began to chant sibilant words, the squid held firmly in her bony fingers.

The old woman's voice grew strangely deep and echoey, and the squid glowed in her hands. Light swirled, growing opaque, and in seconds the door knocker was hidden in a spinning mist, shot through with rainbow colours. The howling wind and rain might as well not have existed for all it affected the spell.

Molly held her breath. The iridescent cloud grew and stretched as Miss Badcrumble chanted to it; soon it was the size of a small person, and still getting bigger. A gust from the cloud itself snatched the door knocker from the Sprye's fingers, but the squid didn't fall to the ground as Molly expected. It hung there in the air, spinning fluidly within the mini-tornado.

When the cloud was as tall as her, Miss Badcrumble gave a little gasp and fell silent, panting. The mist still whirled, hovering above the ground, but as they watched it slowed and solidified, drifting gently to the ground. Molly heard a distinct *thump* as it touched the earth.

The mist dissipated in the wind, the stormy drizzle intensified once more, and the colours faded. And there, where there had been a door knocker no bigger than Molly's hand, stood a huge carved wooden squid, larger than many a human being.

'Miss Badcrumble,' breathed Molly. 'You're brilliant.'

'Why thank you, dear. A little out of breath, but I'll be as right as rain in no time.' Sure enough, the old woman was clutching her chest rather dramatically.

'That should be perfect for your purposes, I think.'

'It's very impressive,' agreed Mason dryly, 'but I still have no idea what Molly's purposes are.'

'We need to get it onto the ship.' Molly gripped a wooden tentacle, testing the weight. 'Can you carry it, Mason?'

'Of course I can.' He gripped the squid securely in his curved claws. 'Nancy and the others should be driving the pirates back to the ship by now, and they'll need our help whether your plan works or not. Climb on board, both of you!'

Molly cupped her hands to give Miss Badcrumble a boost onto Mason's back, then let the old Sprye haul her up in front. No sooner was she settled between his jutting shoulder blades than Mason took to the rain-lashed air once more, easily bearing the weight of the squid as he flew with powerful rhythmic wingbeats towards the open sea.

This time Molly barely had a moment to wonder at the extraordinary view, or the glimmer of a stormy moon against the black water. Her stomach twisted as Mason swooped down and the prow of the *Medusa* reared above them, ominous and threatening, yet strangely naked without its figurehead.

'There!' shouted Molly.

They hurtled towards the prow. Still clasping the squid in one talon, Mason stretched out three of his clawed feet and grasped the jutting bowsprit to halt his flight; Molly felt herself flung forward, and behind her Miss Badcrumble slithered sideways with a squeal of terror.

Wildly Molly grabbed for the old Sprye, seizing her leg mostly by luck. It took all her strength both to keep her own balance, and to steady Miss Badcrumble and haul her back on board. For horrible seconds Molly was sure they would crash together into the black and storm-tossed waves. But as Mason righted himself with a few flaps of his wings, Molly breathed again.

'There, Molly!' There was a light of excited understanding in Mason's eyes at the sight of the empty wooden prow, where Nancy had once been chained. He extended one wing for her to crawl out towards it. 'Quickly, now!'

Gritting her teeth, Molly gripped his wing and began to edge along to the prow. To cling on, she had to dig in her fingers as tight as she could and hope she wasn't hurting him. The sea surged angrily up towards her, crashing against the hull, exploding in white spray. The rain had redoubled its force once more, lashing her face till she could hardly see.

Finally clutching the splintered post, Molly reached back an arm. Now holding on only with his rear claws, Mason stretched forward – Miss Badcrumble squealing on his back, her hands over her eyes – and between them they manoeuvred the great wooden squid into position.

Fumbling blindly, Molly felt her hands slip on wet wood as she seized the dangling chains from which she had so recently freed Nancy. From the shore, over the rumble and crash of thunder and the roar of rain and wind, she could hear the clash of swords, the hollers and howls of battling pirates and gargoyles, drawing closer. Nancy and Arthur were doing their part, then. The rest was up to her.

Oh, please let this work…

The chains swung wildly in the storm, bashing her arms and hands, but she held on grimly, looping the links as best she could around the squid's swirling wooden tentacles. It wasn't perfect, but she'd helped her father with his escapology tricks often enough, and he'd shown her how to secure a chain. With a last mighty tug she pulled the iron links tight around a huge curled tentacle, and snapped the last padlock shut.

Her feet slithered wildly against the soaking hull, and the world spun. She gave a short scream, feeling herself slip; then something grasped her waist, steadying her.

'Mason!' she gasped. 'Thanks!'

'The figurehead is secure, Molly,' he shouted. 'Now, let's get away from here!'

She scrambled up his scaly foreleg, seizing a wing. Miss Badcrumble reached down, leaning perilously, to help Molly haul herself onto the great gargoyle's back. Turning, he took off, veering first wildly towards the surging ship, then rebalancing and flying safely up into the air. The rain lashed them so hard now that it stung Molly's face as she blinked and peered back at the *Medusa*.

A pale and ghastly horde was racing across the waves towards the ship, harried and pursued by the flock of gargoyles. Behind the attackers raced Nancy, yelling in fury at the retreating pirates, slashing with her claws; on her back, Arthur swung at the escaping crew with a broken shard of roof-beam.

'Regroup,' roared the unmistakeable voice of Black Edward Sharksbane. 'Regroup at the *Medusa*, boys, and find more weapons! Then we'll show them who owns their paltry island!'

The ghost pirates were swarming up the ship's sides now, leaping over the gunwales, clambering into the rigging with blades between their teeth. Snarling, they slashed at the harrying gargoyles; the point of a sabre ripped into the stretched skin of a batwing, and the gargoyle squealed with rage and pain.

'The pistols, boys!' yelled Sharksbane, striding across the decks, kicking crates of weaponry into view. 'Haul anchor, Red Peter! Bring her around, Two-Fingers!'

They were going to attack with the ship itself, Molly realised; use the *Medusa* as a gigantic battering ram. From where they soared above the ship, Molly could already see it bucking on the waves as the pirates prepared to charge through the cloud of gargoyles, blades and bullets flashing from the rigging. Mason swerved to avoid the pitching mainmast, and Molly ducked her head to the side too as she felt Miss Badcrumble's arms tighten round her own waist.

'Now,' she cried. 'Miss B, the squid! Bring it to life!'

'Oh! My goodness! Yes!'

Molly didn't dare turn again, but she saw the pink energy crackle once more from the old Sprye's claw-tips. It splintered the night, exploding around the squid and enveloping it in that pale flame.

Molly held her breath as the pirates below stumbled to a halt and stared upwards, stupefied.

'Oh, *please* work, squid!' she whispered.

For what seemed like an age, the squid didn't move, and a single harsh laugh came from one of the pirates. It faded to an uneasy giggle, then he fell silent again.

One tentacle twitched, stretched, uncurled. A vast, black eye blinked open, reflecting the magical flame. The great beak opened, and another suckered arm writhed, touching the ship's timber hull with an experimental tip. Then, with shocking speed, the squid lashed out with all its tentacles, slamming the two longest against the *Medusa's* sides.

From the ship came the tortured screech of wood and iron, and Black Edward, standing on the foredeck, was flung sideways as the *Medusa* lurched.

'Witchcraft!' he screamed as he stumbled to his feet.

Molly clasped her hands over her mouth, clinging on to Mason's back with just her knees, barely able to breathe as the *Medusa* tilted wildly. Black Edward stumbled again, and half a dozen of his crew rolled and tumbled to the starboard side, grabbing at masts and rigging and even loose crates in a hopeless attempt to save themselves.

The squid writhed again and *Medusa*'s stern lurched up suddenly, seawater pouring from it. Despite the rain streaming in her eyes, despite her hair blustering across her face, Molly saw the squid's tentacles reach from the prow and flail towards the surface of the water.

With a great convulsion, the squid released its hold on the hull, and its body pulsated with a surge of violent energy. The *Medusa* swung round helplessly, at the mercy of its own writhing figurehead, tossed and flung by the chained creature as it strained to get back to the deep ocean.

The end, when it came, was very sudden. As if the black sea had opened its jaws and sucked it in, the ship lunged forward and down, first the bowsprit and then the living figurehead diving beneath the waves.

Molly heard the thunderous crack of a hull breaking in half. Ghostly pirates rolled and tumbled towards the foredeck. They were already falling, crashing and shrieking, being sucked one after the other into the black swirling water. Black Edward Sharksbane struggled to climb back up towards the afterdeck, clutching and swinging wildly on torn rigging and ragged sails. He scrambled onto the stern rail, brandishing his cutlass and screaming in blind fury. For an instant the *Medusa* seemed to hesitate, reluctant.

Then, surrendering to the waves, it plunged. As Molly watched, heart in her mouth, the *Medusa* and her captain were swallowed up together in the black waves. Black Edward's echoing roars became gurgles, then faded to a terrible silence as the sea rolled over the empty place where a ship had been, the colossal waves crashing together and subsiding.

Molly found she was clutching so tightly onto Mason's wings, her knuckles were white and her fingers were numb. She flexed them loose, gasping for breath.

'Sorry,' she mumbled.

'That's perfectly all right, Molly.' There was a smile in Mason's gruff voice. He wiggled his wings in relief.

'My goodness,' breathed Miss Badcrumble shakily. 'Oh, my goodness.'

The storm was already dying; the hard rain faded to spatters, and drizzle, and finally to nothing as the wind weakened and became a feeble breeze. Beneath them the huge waves settled, becoming merely choppy and then almost calm. The black clouds parted and dissipated altogether, and the moon shone as clear and bright as the beam from the Ravenstorm Island lighthouse.

Mason watched the water's black surface for a few moments more, then lifted, turned and soared back towards the shore, Nancy at his side and the gargoyle flock following. He landed elegantly on the sand, and Molly slipped gratefully from his back onto solid dry land.

Flying's fantastic, she decided, *but it's just as nice to have your feet on the ground…*

Mason crouched, licking his long teeth as he tested one sabre-wounded wing.

'You're hurt,' exclaimed Molly.

'Only a very little,' he reassured her, 'and worth a small scratch, Molly. That was a clever idea of yours.'

'Indeed.' Nancy plunged onto the sand, trotting a few steps before sinking down at his side. 'An enchanted squid! An inspired thought, Molly.'

'Inspired by Charley,' pointed out Molly. 'I wonder if I'll ever dare tell her.'

'I don't think she'd take it very well,' said Arthur. He dusted sand from his jeans as he walked unsteadily to Miss Badcrumble and helped her down from Mason's back. The old Sprye looked rather shocked, but her cheeks glowed with the excitement of the battle. Around them gargoyles were settling, licking their wounds, flexing their claws and muscles, mewling with pleasure and relief.

'I'll have to buy Jack an extra ice cream,' said Molly. 'He's the one who reminded me squid like to live in deep water.'

'Oh yes. When he drew his picture for Charley!' Arthur smiled. 'Good for Magic Boy.'

'Though…I know they were horrible vandals and everything, but I can't help hoping they're all right down there…' Molly bit her lip as she watched the water's surging surface.

'I'm sure they will be,' said Nancy. 'They're ghosts, remember? Black Edward will be furious, but they won't actually be hurt. The *Medusa* must sail where her figurehead leads her, and the squid will always swim towards the depths. Sharksbane and his crew will sail on forever, Molly, but deep beneath the ocean – where they can't cause any more trouble for Ravenstorm Island!'

'Quite,' said Miss Badcrumble firmly. 'And I don't feel the least bit sorry for them, not after the mess they made of my beautiful museum. Horrid brutes!'

'That reminds me.' Molly swung off her backpack again and dug inside it. 'Here, Miss Badcrumble. I think you're the best person to keep this.'

She laid the compass in Miss Badcrumble's hands, and the old woman gazed down at it.

'Ah, it really is very pretty,' she breathed.

'It could be the centrepiece of your new seafaring collection,' said Arthur. 'After the pirates destroyed the last one.'

'Yes. Yes, it could! There's a lot of damage to the museum, but I'll have it fixed in no time.'

'*We'll* have it fixed,' Nancy corrected her. 'We'll all help, Miss Badcrumble. It's the least we can do; isn't that right, Mason?'

'Indeed.' He nodded solemnly.

Molly glanced at Arthur and grinned. From the wink Arthur gave her, it was clear he too had noticed that as the two gargoyles' claws shimmered and contracted and turned back into human flesh, their fingers were firmly twined together.

Arthur dumped his phone on top of a pile of books in the library, exasperated. 'Honestly, it's useless. I swear that Queen of the Shadowsprye has put a curse on the whole network.'

'I wouldn't be surprised.' Molly laughed. 'I've given up charging mine.'

'Oh well, I'm not too fussed.' Arthur sniffed. 'I'm curious about what George and the gang are getting up to without me, but it's not as if I could tell them all about what I've been doing on the island. Where would I even start? "I saved my cousin from Shadowsprye and then helped my butler battle ghost pirates. And how was your trip to the countryside, Thomas?"'

Behind them the door swung open, and when the two cousins turned at the sound of Mason's cough, he said, 'A visitor for you, Master Arthur and Molly. And particularly for you, Jack…'

'Charley!' Jack dropped his crayons and ran to give his favourite marine biologist a crushing hug. She had to raise the huge paper-wrapped parcel she was carrying above her head, laughing. 'What's the present?' he asked her.

'Jack!' scolded Molly. 'Give Charley ten seconds, why don't you! How's Starfish Cottage, Charley?'

'Much, much better,' smiled Charley as she set down her parcel, then slumped with relief on the arm of the leather sofa. 'I don't know where Mason found all the extra helpers, because he can't have done it on his own and every tradesman on Ravenstorm Island is booked up for weeks. But I've got a new roof and the windows have been replaced already. It's looking wonderful! And I can certainly live in it again.'

'That's the community for you,' remarked Mason solemnly. 'It was my pleasure, Miss Beaumont. That's how we do things on Ravenstorm Island, isn't it?' He left, closing the door softly behind him, but not before Molly had caught his meaningful wink.

Ah-ha! she thought with a grin. *I thought the hall roof looked bare last night. The gargoyles have been helping rebuild Charley's cottage!*

'There's only one thing I never found, and that's my squid door knocker.' Charley shrugged. 'I expect it got swept up with some of the rubble. But I'll just get a new one.'

'It probably went to live at the bottom of the sea,' said Jack, still eyeing the parcel. 'I don't think a squid would like living on somebody's *door*.'

Arthur had to clap his hand over his mouth to muffle a snort of laughter, and Molly thumped him on the back, turning her cousin's laughter into a cough.

'Oh, Charley!' she said loudly. 'We forgot to return your spare boat keys. Here you go!'

'Ah! Thanks, Molly.' Charley narrowed her eyes at them. 'Well, I don't know what you two have been up to with your weather studies, but it's brightened up no end, so you must be miracle workers!'

'Yes,' sighed Arthur. 'No more storms. Back to regular mist and drizzle.'

Molly grinned. 'We're just lucky, I guess.'

'I wish you'd open that present,' grumbled Jack.

Charley laughed. 'It's not a toy, Jack, and it's for everybody. It's a thank you for having me to stay. But go on, open it!'

Jack needed no second asking. He tore off the paper, sending shreds of it flying, and gasped as he tugged the lid off the box. 'It's a ship!'

'Oh,' exclaimed Molly. 'It's beautiful!'

It was a fully-masted and rigged galleon in miniature, bigger than Jack's whole arm-span – which became obvious when he tried to lift it. Molly clasped him and drew him gently away.

'Whoa, don't touch, Jack! Remember what Charley said – it's not a toy. And it's for Aunt Catherine and Uncle Bill, too!'

'What is?' Aunt Catherine smiled from the doorway. 'Oh, Charley! How lovely to see you again.'

'Look, Mum.' Arthur swivelled the delicately beautiful ship on its stand. 'Charley's brought us this!'

'Oh my,' breathed Catherine, gently touching the tiny glass windows, the silken furled sails, the intricate paintwork of the figurehead. 'You didn't have to do that, Charley – it was a pleasure having you here – but thank you! It's stunning. About eighteen-ninety, I'd say?' She bent to examine the hull, peering into the miniature stern cabin.

'Eighteen-eighties,' said Uncle Bill confidently, appearing at her side with Harriet in his arms. He laid the baby gently down, fast asleep, in her travel cot beside the sofa. 'I'm familiar with the maker's work. He's very well known on the mainland. What a splendid gift, Charley!'

'It was pretty splendid of *you* to put me up.' Charley grinned.

'You must stay for tea, Charley,' smiled Catherine. 'There's carrot cake. With cream-cheese icing.'

'Yes you *must*!' agreed Jack, grabbing Charley's hand and pulling her down into a deep squashy armchair. He snatched up a fistful of crayons. 'I'll draw you another squid. To make up for your door knocker.'

'Well… That would be lovely, Jack. And I'd love to stay for tea.' Charley grinned. 'If you're making it.'

'It's already made,' said a new voice.

Nancy winked at Molly and Arthur as she carried the tea tray into the library. There was no sign now of her gargoyle self: her face glowed with the heat from the kitchen and her glossy red hair was pulled back into a sleek ponytail. She looked warm and elegant and entirely human.

For now, thought Molly with an inward smile.

'Charley, this is our new housekeeper, Nancy,' Uncle Bill introduced them. 'It turns out she came with the house just like Mason did. You've been on holiday, though – isn't that right, Nancy?'

'Indeed,' said Nancy with a secret smile at Molly and Art. 'I was on a cruise.'

'The cake looks fantastic, Nancy.' Molly stifled her grin.

'I'm very glad. Now, Mason needs a hand with the creeper outside the ground floor rooms. It's affecting the pointing and it needs clearing. Just call me if you need anything!'

When Nancy had smiled her farewells and left the

library, Aunt Catherine puffed out a bewildered breath and shook her head. 'Mason is such a dark horse, isn't he, Bill? I had no idea he had a wife. You know, Charley, she only reappeared the other day. Out of nowhere!'

'I think he just plays his hand very close to his chest, Mum,' Arthur told her solemnly.

'Nancy seems very nice,' ventured Charley.

'Oh, she *is*,' chorused the two cousins together.

'All the same, aren't couples funny?' Aunt Catherine wrinkled her nose in slight perplexity. 'He's such a strange man – quite brooding – and Nancy's so very pretty…'

'Oh, Mum.' Arthur rolled his eyes. 'I think they have quite a lot in common, actually.'

'Oh yes, dear, I'm sure you're right. Now, shall I pour?'

They were interrupted by a squalling cry from Harriet, curling her fists and blinking awake.

'Looks like I'd better handle this,' said Uncle Bill, taking the teapot from Catherine's hands.

'And you'd better handle that…'

'Don't worry, Mum, I'll settle her,' said Arthur confidently.

'Would you? Oh thank you, Art. She doesn't seem to respond to me these days.' Aunt Catherine sounded tired and rather sad as she subsided onto the sofa.

Giving her aunt a concerned look, Molly joined Arthur as he reached down into the travel cot to lift Harriet. The baby's eyes were screwed as tight as her fists as she grizzled in her big brother's arms.

'Mum says the doctor isn't worried at all,' said Arthur in a low voice. 'We're to keep an eye on her but he reckons it's quite normal. She's just growing a bit faster than a regular baby.'

'She really doesn't seem very happy, though, does she?' Molly sighed and tickled Harriet's miniature toes, but the baby only squirmed and wailed miserably. She batted at Molly's hand and her tiny fingers grabbed on tight to Molly's. 'Wow, she really is developing fast. Babies can't normally grip things until they're a couple of months old.'

'Really?' Arthur frowned.

Molly nodded. 'Jack learned to cling on to things when he was three months old. I remember he got hold of Mum's magic wand somehow and wouldn't let it go. He kept hitting Dad with it.'

'Wow, so she's really growing superfast! Is it hard being a baby genius, then? Come on, sis, give us a smile,' coaxed Arthur, taking Harriet's tiny hand and tickling it.

Grumpily, Harriet opened her eyes at last. And both Arthur and Molly gasped in shock.

The baby's eyes had been dark slate-blue the last time Molly had seen her awake. Not any more. The irises glowed orange, and the pupils were slitted, like a cat's.

'What on earth?' whispered Arthur. Clutching his baby sister even more tightly, he hurriedly turned his back on his mother, concealing Harriet in case Aunt Catherine glanced over. 'Molly!' he hissed. 'What's happened to my sister?'

Molly swallowed hard and touched Harriet's

downy cheek. The baby had quietened now, and she gazed at Molly with an intense, unflinching, golden-orange stare.

'I barely want to think it,' she whispered. 'But maybe…she's growing superfast for a reason.'

Little Harriet squeezed her eyes tight shut in a baby-scowl. When they blinked open once more, she gave them the normal, slightly vague blue gaze of a human baby.

'Molly.' Arthur took a breath, then swallowed with difficulty. 'We didn't imagine that, did we?'

'No.' Molly shook her head, frightened.

'I know one thing,' muttered Arthur. 'Whatever's wrong with Harriet, it isn't normal.'

'Something magic is happening to her,' Molly's throat felt dry and tight. 'Maybe something bad.'

'Yes,' agreed Arthur unhappily. 'Magic. And that only means one thing, Molly.'

Molly nodded. 'That it's up to us, Art. Something on Ravenstorm Island has put a spell on Harriet, and we're going to have to find out what, and why. Don't worry, Harriet,' she whispered to the squirming baby in Arthur's arms. 'We'll find a way to put this right.'

Don't miss Molly and Arthur's first adventure on
Ravenstorm Island!

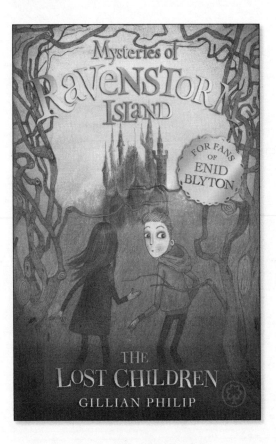

A gust of wind sliced a hole through the mist. Below, a rugged shape jutted out of the sea, like a monster coming up for air. Molly Cornell grinned.

'There, Jack!' she said. 'Ravenstorm Island, look!'

'Where? Let me see!'

Her little brother unsnapped his seatbelt and scrambled across her to peer out of the plane window.

'Oof! Watch where you're putting your foot…'

'Best to keep your seatbelt on, young man,' called the pilot over his shoulder.

'You heard him.' Molly wrestled the grumbling Jack back into his seat. 'Don't worry, we'll be seeing it up close soon enough.'

'I didn't see the airport,' Jack objected.

'You won't. There isn't one! Mum and Dad said you can't get to Ravenstorm Island except on this seaplane. Or a boat, but the harbour's tiny, too.'

'Cool,' breathed Jack. 'I want to see the harbour.' He reached for his seatbelt clasp again.

'Stay there!' Exasperated, Molly held him down with one hand and fumbled in her pocket with the other. 'Show you a trick?'

'If it's a good one.' Jack folded his arms.

Molly drew out a ten-pence piece and held it between her fingertips. 'Bazooka!' She waved her other hand across the coin, closing her eyes as if in a trance. 'And – gone!' She opened her empty hand.

Jack shut one eye critically. 'Now bring it back.'

Molly stroked her fist and opened her fingers, the coin nestling in her palm once again. 'Ta-dah!'

Jack rolled his eyes, unimpressed. 'That's a French Drop. Easy-peasy. Mum showed me. Now make it go through your head.'

Smothering a grin, Molly flipped the coin back

to her fingertips. 'OK, then…'

When her parents got back from their summer tour, she'd have to ask them to show her some different magic tricks. Jack was getting mighty picky for a four-year-old. Any minute now he'd demand that she saw someone in half. It would have to be their only fellow-passenger on the tiny plane – that boy in the expensive-looking school uniform. He hadn't spoken once since they'd boarded the plane, just read his book or stared out of the window. Molly wondered if he was visiting relatives on Ravenstorm Island, as she and Jack were.

Like most summers, Molly and Jack would be spending this one apart from their parents – the Incredible Cornells were in huge demand at resorts and hotels throughout the holiday season – but this would be the first year she and Jack had spent with the Wolfreys at Ravenstorm Hall. Molly didn't remember Uncle Bill and Aunt Catherine, and Jack had never met them. Bill and Catherine only had a son, Art – short for Arthur – who was the same age as Molly, so there wouldn't be anyone for Jack to play with. Molly had a feeling that without a few new tricks to show him, it was going to be a long summer. Now, if only she could do *real* magic…

Sure enough, Jack was fidgeting again, his fingers straying towards his seatbelt clasp.

'Jack, stop that. Look – don't get out of your seat, you'll be able to see sitting down! The plane's banking. Now! The whole island's right there. See?'

Wow, Molly thought. She hoped Jack was as impressed as she was. The island might be small, but from up here it looked like a whole other world. The sea was azure, dazzling even through the clinging tendrils of mist, and it fringed the sandy coves with tiny white waves. Narrow streets wound through a village that hugged the harbour, picture-book pretty, its houses built of a warm yellow-grey stone. She could make out a church spire, a white lighthouse along the cliffs, and beyond that, a vast stone mansion with turrets and crow-stepped gables that edged the roof like tiny staircases.

From one wing rose an impressive round tower.

'Whoa!' said Jack, mouth agape. 'Molly, look at the castle!'

'It's amazing, isn't it? And those gardens.' From up high, the lawns and hedges looked as if they'd been trimmed with tiny scissors into their elaborate designs. Molly had never seen so many different shades of patterned green. As the plane turned again, and sunlight flashed off its wing, she could make out deep woods behind the mansion, mysterious and enticing. Their low flight startled a horde of ravens, which took off from the mansion's treetops in alarm.

'Ravenstorm Hall,' murmured Molly. 'Has to be!'

'I'm going to like it,' declared Jack.

Well, that's good news, Molly thought with an inward smile. Once Jack was determined about something, there was no backtracking. He'd like their summer home now if it killed him.